HARLEQUIN®

SUPERROMANCE

D0051649

TWO SISTERS

Kay David

Twins

HARLEQUIN®
Makes any time special ™

ISBN 0-373-70888-2

50450

AVAILABLE NOW:

"I'd be happy to look into your sister's disappearance."

Elizabeth's eyes widened in surprise. "Oh, no. Please. That's not why I told you about it."

"I know, but I don't mind. I can check some things Missing Persons might not get around to so fast." *If ever.*

"I appreciate it, but…" Rising from the bench, Elizabeth ran a hand over her jacket, as if ensuring that her defensive shell was still in place. "I really can't ask you to do that."

John's curiosity got the better of him, and he decided to push her to find out why she wouldn't allow herself to accept his offer. "I want to help you. Why won't you let me?"

She blinked. "April will turn up sooner or later," she said in a stilted voice. "It's not that I don't appreciate your offer, but I don't want to involve you in our personal problems."

Something in the way she spoke took his curiosity to another level. "You have some personal problems?"

Her gaze didn't waver. "Doesn't everyone?"

He didn't answer, but let the silence build. Most people felt uncomfortable with silence. He found out all kinds of things when they tried to fill the void. Elizabeth simply stared at him—which told him even more about her.…

ABOUT THE AUTHOR

Ranging from the deeply emotional to the dark and dangerous, Kay David's stories frequently take place in one of the many exotic locations where she and Pieter, her husband of twenty-five years, have resided, including the Middle East and South America. Currently, Kay and Pieter have come back home to live with their much-beloved cat, Leroy, on the Gulf Coast of Texas.

Books by Kay David

HARLEQUIN SUPERROMANCE

798—THE ENDS OF THE EARTH
823—ARE YOU MY MOMMY?
848—THE MAN FROM HIGH MOUNTAIN

TWO SISTERS
Kay David

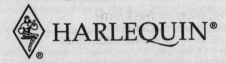

HARLEQUIN®

TORONTO • NEW YORK • LONDON
AMSTERDAM • PARIS • SYDNEY • HAMBURG
STOCKHOLM • ATHENS • TOKYO • MILAN • MADRID
PRAGUE • WARSAW • BUDAPEST • AUCKLAND

ISBN 0-373-70888-2

TWO SISTERS

Copyright © 2000 by Carla Luan.

Visit us at www.romance.net

Printed in U.S.A.

TWO SISTERS

CHAPTER ONE

"I DANCE AND men pay money to watch." April Benoit glared at her sister, her expression tight in the growing darkness, her voice tense. "What right do you have to hassle me over this? *You,* of all people?"

Standing in the living room of her Houston town house, Elizabeth Benoit met April's angry stare. Their eyes were so similar it was like looking into a mirror. But beyond the physical resemblances, nothing else about them was the same—from the way they thought to the way they dressed. It'd been different in the past; they'd been so connected, they could finish each other's sentences. Now they were opposites, and Elizabeth often wondered how they could even be sisters, much less identical twins. She spoke quietly, her demeanor calmer than she felt.

"I have that right because I love you and I only want what's best for you."

"Well, what's best for me is eating! And if I don't work, I don't eat." April's beautiful eyes narrowed. "As I recall, there was a time when you depended on me for that, as well, or have you forgotten?''

"I haven't for—"

"Good! Then leave me alone and let me make a living the way I want to."

Elizabeth said patiently, "There are a lot of ways to make money, April. Dancing isn't—"

April cut her off. "Gosh, you mean I could be a brain surgeon? All these years, I could have been operating on people and making a bundle, instead of taking my clothes off?" She made a sound of disgust. "Get real, Elizabeth! I wasn't lucky enough to finish school like you."

"Luck had nothing to do with it. It was hard work, okay? You could have done it, too." Elizabeth shook her head, exasperation finally edging its way inside her at the turn the conversation was taking. "You could go back to school right now, for God's sake. There's plenty of time. You're still young."

"Young! Yeah, right." April rolled her eyes. "Twenty-eight isn't old?"

"Only dancers think that's old, but it's not. And even if it was, it's never too late for a new start."

April rose abruptly from the sofa where she'd been sitting and crossed to the window. Her back to Elizabeth, she stared out at the street. It was another hot Texas evening. The summer sun had just fallen below the horizon, but streaks of red and orange still colored the sky.

"You don't understand," she said plaintively. "You just don't understand."

At her sister's tone, Elizabeth's irritation turned to sympathy. She'd been about to turn on a lamp, but instead moved quickly to April's side and put a hand on her arm. "I *do* understand, and you know it, but you could get out," she said. "If you wanted to…"

"I like dancing." Without meeting Elizabeth's eyes, April spoke into the night. "I like the money. I like the people…"

"You like the peop—" Elizabeth broke off, shaking her head and dropping her hand. "How can you say that, April? Look at Tracy! You're *her* friend—you help her out and do things for her—but she isn't yours. She'd stab you in the back and never give it a second thought. And Greg! Is he really the kind of man you want to spend your life with?"

"Tracy's okay, and Greg gave me a job when I needed one. Don't knock him."

"Any idiot with eyes in his head would have given you a job. You're gorgeous! You're smart! Sweetheart, c'mon! You could be doing anything you want to if you'd just—"

April whirled around, eyes flashing, hands balled into fists. "Goddamn it, Elizabeth, get off my case!'' she yelled. ''For once just leave me alone, would you?''

Elizabeth stepped back, the room humming with April's startling fury. ''Sweetheart, I'm concerned. I was only—''

''—poking your nose into my business like you have ever since Dad died. I'm not a kid, Elizabeth, and I don't need somebody taking care of me all the time. I'm not Mom, okay?''

Elizabeth immediately blanked her expression to hide her hurt, but the words cut deeply, painfully. When they were twelve, they'd lost their father—a euphemism Elizabeth hated but used out of habit— and she'd taken care of herself and April and had pulled them through the disaster with their mother that had followed. Not because Elizabeth wanted to but because she'd had to. Their mother, a fragile woman, had depended on her husband so completely that when he died...well, what had happened to *him* had been less painful by far.

She pointed out none of this.

''I'm sorry,'' she said, instead, her voice stiff. ''I thought I was helping.''

April paused, then took a deep breath, the line of her jaw tightening. ''Well, you aren't. I'm not perfect like you. And I never will be, so stop trying to make me that way, okay?''

Elizabeth's mouth dropped open in surprise. ''Perfect? That's ridiculous. I'm not perfect! And I never meant to make you like me. Is…is that what you think?''

"I don't know what to think, but I do know you've been trying to run my life for years, and I'm sick and tired of it. I just want to be myself, do things my own way."

"Being yourself is what you should be, April. I only—''

April held up her hand, her bloodred nails gleaming in the dying light. "Drop it, Elizabeth! Let me make my own mistakes. *Leave me alone.*''

To Elizabeth it seemed as if a chasm had opened between them even though she hadn't moved an inch from her stance at the window. She felt it deep down inside and it sent a cold chill skittering down her back. The closeness they'd once shared was gone forever.

IT WAS EARLY DAWN, and the sky was a pearly white tinged with blue and pink. The late-summer moon still hung above the horizon, a cool white disk, barely visible, while at the same time, the sun had begun to peek over the neighbor's roof. The scent of gardenias lay thick in the humid air, and the manicured emerald lawns, stretching out before him, shimmered with dew.

John Mallory stood in the open door of his town house and looked around, a mug of hot coffee steaming in his hand. He always began the day this way, staring out at the street, soaking in the serenity—wondering just what kind of disaster the hours ahead would bring. As a Houston cop he'd seen just about everything, but some days could still surprise him.

He was about to take another sip of coffee when he caught a sudden movement in his peripheral vision. His gut tightened automatically when he realized who he was seeing. It was his neighbor, Elizabeth Benoit, walking to her car. He knew her name only because he'd seen it on her mailbox. She didn't speak to him or to anyone else as far as he could tell. She was leaving earlier than usual this morning, her stride hurried yet graceful, her black hair gleaming, her dark eyes already hidden behind sunglasses. She was one of those incredibly beautiful women, like his ex-wife Marsha, who noticed people only when she needed them.

And that was damned seldom.

His phone sounded, and John stepped back into the house, slamming the door behind him. Just as well, he thought, crossing the living room and heading down the hall to the kitchen. He was an idiot for even noticing Elizabeth Benoit. Dazzling women were always trouble, and trouble like that he definitely did not need. A few years before, he had disentangled himself from one such woman—and he still had the scars to prove it.

As if he needed further incentive to remember

that, the voice on the other end of the line provided a sharp reminder.

"John. This is Marsha. Look, I only have a minute, but I wanted to catch you before I left for work. I've got a problem with this week."

John deliberately placed his coffee cup into the sink before he answered. His ex-wife didn't believe in such niceties as saying hello. She was always in a hurry and looking for ways to streamline her life. He couldn't understand why; what did she do with all that extra time?

"What's the problem, Marsha?" he asked as pleasantly as he could.

"Lisa has to get her hair trimmed and the only time Luis can do it is Thursday evening, and you know I have to be there. I'm sorry, but you can have her next week as usual."

John counted to three before he spoke. "Our arrangement is for me to have our daughter *every* Thursday. You'll have to take her to the beauty shop some other day."

"But Luis only had that time open."

"She's five years old, Marsha." Again he waited a beat, looked out the kitchen window at a crow pecking at something on the sidewalk. "She doesn't need to go to the most expensive hairdresser in town to have her bangs trimmed."

Her voice turned hostile. "John, if you want to hassle me about something this minor, we can go back to court. I'd be more than happy to accommodate you, and we can work out a few other details, too...."

She droned on and John tuned her out. Marsha hadn't always been difficult, and once upon a time, they'd really been in love. Somewhere down the line, though, he'd disappointed her and she'd turned bitter. When at last she paused to draw a breath, he broke in, his words clipped and precise so they wouldn't reveal his desire to reach through the phone and throttle her.

"Marsha, I will be there Thursday at five to pick up our daughter. I will keep her overnight, then I will bring her back Friday morning when I go to work, just as I do every week. Find another time to get her hair cut. Goodbye."

Marsha was still talking when he hung up the phone.

He headed for his bedroom shaking his head and thought of Elizabeth Benoit once more. She was a gorgeous woman, but if being married to one for six long years hadn't taught him how dangerous such women were, he was a fool. And the realization that he was generalizing didn't bother him a bit. Beautiful women were his weakness, and he'd dated enough of them to know what he was talking about.

WHEN ELIZABETH woke up and stumbled outside for the paper, all she knew was that April was gone.

After their horrible fight, they'd gone to bed, Elizabeth to her room, April to the guest room Elizabeth always kept ready for her. Elizabeth had tossed and turned for hours, her worry about April keeping her awake. Now April was gone—and so was Elizabeth's car.

As she stared at the empty spot by the curb where the car had been the night before, she asked herself why she was even surprised. This was typical. April acted as if she were a teenager, totally self-absorbed and interested in nothing beyond her own tiny world. Didn't she know how much she worried Elizabeth? Elizabeth tried to stem the flow of resentment, but it bubbled over, hot and bitter. Was she doomed to always be the caretaker and April the one who lived life only for herself?

A car drove by and honked. Snatching up the newspaper, Elizabeth stepped back inside and closed the door. A vague feeling of guilt swept over her. Had she been so busy working to get away from the life she and April had shared that she'd neglected April somehow? Remembering April's angry retorts last night, Elizabeth answered herself immediately. She'd done all she could and more—and look at the thanks she'd got!

Elizabeth dropped the *Chronicle* on the table in the entry and headed for her bedroom to dress for work, flipping on the stereo as she passed it.

Still seething, she dressed quickly, pinned back

her hair and slapped on a minimum of makeup. She needed this extra hassle as much as she needed another headache, and she had plenty of those even without April's help. She didn't trust April's clunker, still parked outside, to get her downtown, so she called the limo company. As she waited, she gulped a cup of instant coffee and punched in the phone number at April's apartment. After the tenth ring she hung up. Her sister didn't even have an answering machine.

Elizabeth tried to check her anger, but the emotion only grew. Deep down, she knew why. She was acting out the part she'd always played, just as April was. April would do something foolish, then Elizabeth would get angry and worried. They'd make up, then the dance would begin all over again. They knew their respective roles well, Elizabeth thought, shaking her head in disgust. Too well.

Twenty minutes later she walked into her office, determined to focus on her job. It was what people paid her for. Betty Starnes, her secretary, greeted her as she opened the door.

"Oh, good morning, Elizabeth. Did you have a nice birthday celebration?"

Elizabeth groaned. "Not really." With as little detail as possible, she explained the situation while Betty nodded in sympathy. She'd been with Elizabeth for years, so she understood completely.

"And you still haven't heard from her?"

Elizabeth tamped down a knot of anxiety. "Not a word. So, if she calls…"

"I'll put her through immediately, don't worry."

Elizabeth entered her office. As a consulting tax attorney, her practice ran the gamut from financial planning to settling estates. Lately most of her cases had been coming from the federal government. She was fast earning a reputation for being able to uncover the most clever of frauds, and with the government attorneys overworked and underpaid, more and more work was being sent to attorneys like her. Just the previous week she'd received a file involving a woman named Linda Tremont and her brother, Tony Masterson. They owned a family investment firm, and several of the investors had complained to the S.E.C. Mainly elderly people, most felt something was wrong with their accounts, because the only one making any money seemed to be Masterson. When Elizabeth had made the initial call to Masterson's office, Linda Tremont had answered, explaining that she was in charge of the firm and her brother primarily gathered new accounts. Tremont was cooperating fully and appeared horrified there could be a problem. She was a leader in Houston's high society, Elizabeth knew. She chaired all the galas and raised incredible amounts of money for the local art scene. How awful to have a brother and business partner who might ruin their family name. From what Elizabeth had seen so far, Anthony Masterson seemed as irresponsible as April.

With a heavy sigh Elizabeth opened the file and began to work.

Hours later, when she took off her glasses and rubbed her eyes, Elizabeth was shocked to see the time. Almost six! The day had disappeared, and she still hadn't heard from April. Elizabeth quickly dialed her sister's number, but just as before, the line rang emptily. Her worry rising once more, she pulled out her address book, looked up the number of the place on Richmond Avenue where April danced, then punched in the number.

"Esquire Club." The husky female voice that answered on the third ring was one Elizabeth recognized. She'd talked to Tracy on the phone several times, and they'd met once in person. Elizabeth had recognized Tracy's type immediately, and she'd tried to warn her sister, but as usual April had blown off the advice. Red-haired and curvaceous, Tracy Kensington had been the most popular dancer at the club—until April's arrival. In that business, the younger the girl, the better the tips, and Tracy was a few years older than April. To make up for that she vied with April for the top spot, the best time, the hottest music. Despite that, April had always been friendly toward her and still was, but Tracy didn't return the favor. Every time she had a chance, she tried to sabotage April.

"Tracy, this is Elizabeth Benoit, April's sister. I was wondering if you've seen April today?"

"Haven't seen her," Tracy replied, her west-Texas drawl replacing some of the sexy purr but not all of it. "Your sister gone missin'?"

"She's not missing. I just can't get an answer at her place. She works tonight, doesn't she?"

"I guess so."

"What time is she supposed to be there?"

"I'm not sure."

Elizabeth tried to stifle her irritation. The dancers were all very tight-lipped, not just to people who weren't part of the life, but among themselves; there wasn't a lot of sharing. Elizabeth suspected that it was simply a result of the competitiveness of the work, each dancer playing her cards close to her chest so as not to give anyone else an edge. It did not, however, make Elizabeth's situation less frustrating. She was April's sister, for God's sake, not some weirdo stranger.

She kept the annoyance from her voice. "Could I talk to Mr. Lansing, then, please?"

Without replying, the woman dropped the phone and walked away—Elizabeth could hear her high heels clacking on the hard floor at the club. Then she heard Tracy call out, "Greg! You there? Phone call!"

Elizabeth tapped her pen against her desk impatiently. After an interminable wait, Greg Lansing, the manager of the club, picked up the phone and said hello. His voice was as gravelly as Tracy's, but raspier, the result, Elizabeth was sure, of too many years of booze, cigarettes and shouting over hundred-decibel rock music for hours at a time. They'd never met, but she'd seen him one night when she'd worn glasses and a scarf and sneaked into the club to watch April dance.

Elizabeth could see why April found him attractive. Tall and well built, he had long blond hair and radiated the kind of bad-boy attitude some women found really appealing. Not Elizabeth. She'd met too many men just like him, and she could easily recognize the sleaze beneath the thin veneer of handsomeness.

"Mr. Lansing, this is Elizabeth Benoit. I'm looking for April."

"Haven't seen her." His voice started fading even before he finished speaking. She realized he was about to hang up.

"Wait—wait, Mr. Lansing! Please…"

There was a second's silence and she thought she'd lost him. Then he said, "What?"

"What time is she due in tonight?"

"I don't keep track of when the different girls come on." She heard him pull on a cigarette. "Probably around twelve, one. Something like that." Above the clink of glasses and laughter, music throbbed in the background. An old Aerosmith hit, the bass rumbling out with a downbeat rhythm.

He was lying, of course. He kept track of everything at the club, down to the last penny and the closing minute. She ignored his prevarication and concentrated on finding out more. "I thought April was more than just one of the girls to you."

He hesitated for a moment, then his voice went into an even lower-pitched growl. "Your sister's a nutcase. I'm trying to stay away from her, and if you had any sense, you would, too."

Elizabeth tensed. "What are you talking about?"

"April's gettin' into some bad shit. She don't watch out, she's gonna be in some serious trouble." Again he drew on the cigarette, the sound harsh in her ear. "The kind of trouble that hurts. Permanently."

Elizabeth's fingers stilled, her pen clattering to the desk. "What are you saying? What's going on with April?"

"She's *your* sister. Ask her if you wanna know." He paused and drew yet again on the cigarette, this time even more deeply. As though she were standing in the darkened club beside him, Elizabeth could almost feel the music, almost smell the smoke.

When he spoke, his voice was so full of warning Elizabeth shivered. "But don't wait too long to ask her, or you might lose your chance."

SHE WORRIED until she could stand it no longer. Late that night, she gave in and called the police. The woman who took the information was polite, but just barely. They covered the basics—name, address, age—then she asked a few more questions.

"How long has your sister been gone?"

"I saw her last night. She slept at my place, but this morning, when I got up, she had left."

"Less than twenty-four hours...." The woman spoke as if to herself, obviously filling out some kind of report.

"Does that matter?" Elizabeth asked anxiously. "Does she have to be gone a certain length of time before you'll start looking?"

"No. That's just on TV. We'll start looking immediately if it's a serious report."

"And what makes it serious?"

"Suspicious circumstances, primarily. Do you have cause to believe something's wrong?"

Elizabeth bit her bottom lip.

"Ma'am?"

"I don't know for sure that anything's happened to her, but I'm worried. I mean Houston's a dangerous place, right?"

"But do you have a specific reason to believe she might have been harmed?"

"Well, her boss—he's an ex-boyfriend—told me she might be getting into serious trouble. He wouldn't say more."

"And he is...?"

Elizabeth spelled out Greg Lansing's name, then in a halting voice, told the woman where he worked.

"He runs the Esquire Club? And your sister works there?"

"What difference does that make?" Elizabeth heard the defensiveness in her voice.

The woman on the other end of the phone hesitated. "Well, it does put a different spin on things, doesn't it?"

"You mean if she ran an oil company, you'd start looking for her, but since she's an exotic dancer, you'll give it a few days first?"

"I mean, Ms. Benoit, some people have more stable lifestyles than others. It's more significant when they disappear because of that. Has your sister ever done this type of thing before?"

Elizabeth closed her eyes. "Yes," she said quietly. "About two years ago. She went to the Caribbean for a week without telling me." With a man she didn't know. She'd sent Elizabeth a postcard, but then at the end of the week, she'd called Elizabeth collect. Crying and desperate, she said the man had abandoned her. He'd turned out to be different than she'd thought was her only explanation. Elizabeth had sent her money for the fare home, and April had assured her of one thing—she would never disappear that way again. She promised she'd tell Elizabeth if she was leaving town, and she had done so faithfully.

Until now.

Elizabeth tried to explain but she could almost hear the investigator's mind slam shut.

"Why don't you give it a few more days, Ms. Benoit? If you haven't heard from your sister by Tuesday or so, then call us back. That would probably be the best way to handle this."

Elizabeth thanked the woman and hung up. There was nothing else she could do.

CHAPTER TWO

JOHN STOOD in the breezeway of the town homes Wednesday evening, by the mailboxes, and watched old Mrs. LeBlanc totter away, a polite smile plastered on his face as he asked himself, for the umpteenth time, why he didn't just move. The place had a few people his age, but most of the residents were ancient tiny women who were constantly trying to fix him up with divorced grandnieces or granddaughters who had five kids. Before he'd come here—after Marsha had gotten the house—he'd lived in an apartment, an anonymous place where no one spoke to anyone. Then his mother had passed away and left him the town house. It'd seemed easier to move in than to sell the place, and it *was* in a safe neighborhood. He never worried about bringing Lisa over.

There were the little old ladies, though, and women like Elizabeth Benoit to contend with. He took two steps and was tossing the junk mail from his box into the nearest trash container when the woman in question came around the corner.

She had her briefcase in one hand and her purse

in the other. Tucked under one arm was a dark blue
folder with the words "Benoit Consulting—Personal and Confidential" printed on the outside in
silver script. His eyes went to Elizabeth herself. Her
dark gold suit, like the black one she'd had on the
last time he'd seen her, looked as though it'd been
made for her, the jacket hugging her figure—but not
too tightly—and the skirt ending at a tantalizing
point just above her knees. The color was just right
for her, her ivory skin glowing from its reflection,
reminding him of his mother's translucent plates
still sitting in the china cabinet in his dining room.
Everything about Elizabeth Benoit was polished,
perfect and gorgeous—except for the ferocious
frown marring her forehead.

Seeing John, she pulled up short. Her frown van-
ished and was replaced with studied politeness.

Normally he would have nodded, turned on his
heel and left, but instead he stood and stared at her.
She was the first to break eye contact. John told
himself to walk away, but his feet seemed fixed to
the sidewalk. She leaned past him and unlocked her
mailbox. Her key ring, he noticed, had a Mercedes-
Benz symbol on it. She reached inside but her fingers came out empty—she hadn't even received the
junk mail he had. When she straightened, she looked
so crushed he spoke without thinking.

"No mail?"

She lifted her gaze, and he was shocked into silence. A smart-aleck reply, a cold shoulder, even a curt go-to-hell wouldn't have surprised him as much as the sight of her exquisite dark eyes filling with tears.

Before he could react, Mrs. Beetleman from 10D came around the corner. She glanced curiously at Elizabeth, then turned her twenty-thousand-dollar face to John and seemed about to speak. Nodding quickly, John engineered their escape, taking Elizabeth's elbow and leading her away before the old woman could ask what was wrong.

They crossed to a nearby iron bench, which was shaded by a huge pin oak. Elizabeth Benoit sat down heavily, and John, shielding her from Mrs. Beetleman's puzzled stare, took the seat beside her, pulling his handkerchief from his pocket and handing it to her. She nodded her thanks and dabbed her eyes.

When she finished, she stared at the square of white cotton for a second, then finally looked up. "I haven't seen a man with a real handkerchief in his pocket since my father died."

Her voice was a throaty contralto and it washed over John with a heavy warmth. "I'm a cop," he said without thinking. "Always gotta be prepared."

She nodded as if his ridiculous answer made perfect sense. For a moment they sat side by side in the hot twilight. The traffic noise on the side street and the cries of children playing in the neighborhood park kept the moment from the awkwardness of total silence.

Finally he spoke. "Is there something I can do for you? You look upset."

To his horror, her eyes filled up again. She shook her head, then answered unexpectedly, her voice huskier than before, the words tight and angry. "It's my sister," she said. "I can't find her. I thought she might have at least sent me a postcard."

"Are you saying she's missing?"

She nodded. "Yes. She came over to my place for a birthday celebration. Then we…we had an argument and I haven't seen her since. And I'm really worried." She looked down at her hands and shook her head, speaking again, this time softly. "I can't believe I'm telling you this." She made a motion as if to get up. "I'm sorry—I shouldn't be bothering you…"

He reached out and put his hand on her arm. She seemed startled by the touch and he instantly pulled back, but not before his brain had registered the sensation. Skin so warm and soft it was sinful. "Please…don't leave. Tell me."

She hesitated, then after a moment she sank back down to the bench. "I know you're a policeman. Mrs. Shaftel told me."

She blinked suddenly, as if she'd given away a secret. And maybe she had, he thought. She'd obviously had a conversation about him with her neighbor. Did that mean she'd been as aware of him as he was of her?

She spoke again, quickly this time. "What kind of cop are you?"

"I'm a detective," he answered. "Homicide."

She nodded, almost to herself.

"How old is your sister?" he asked. "Is she a juvenile?"

"No...no." She shook her head. "She's my age. We're twins, identical twins. We turned twenty-eight on Sunday."

Warning bells sounded in his head. Twenty-eight. What was he thinking? His thirty-seven suddenly seemed ancient. He was surprised she hadn't called him sir. It always killed him when they did that.

"Twenty-eight," he repeated. "So she's an adult. No runaway situation. Maybe she took a trip. Went somewhere for a while and just didn't say anything to you."

"She'd tell me first, probably even borrow money from me." She licked her lips, then pulled her bottom one in between her teeth. "She took my car, too."

He kept his expression neutral. "You could file a stolen vehicle report."

"I don't want to do that." Her voice was stronger now, more in control. He could see the shell of her usual demeanor coming back into place. "I've reported her missing. That's all I'm going to do. I don't want her hauled in or anything.''

He shrugged. ''Might be the easiest way to find her.''

''No.''

No further explanation, no other words to back it up. Just ''no.''

''Does she live with you? I don't think I've seen her around.''

''She has her own apartment at The Pines. On lower Montrose.'' She sent him a quick glance, then looked back down at her hands. Lower Montrose was a long way from where they sat—not in miles but in financial terms. It wasn't the best part of Houston. ''She works...over by the Galleria.''

John waited a moment, then spoke again. ''Do you think she's in trouble?''

Her eyes jerked to his, the gaze narrowing. ''Why do you ask?''

''You're awfully worried.''

''Wouldn't you be if your sister had disappeared?''

For one short moment his muscles in his chest tightened painfully, making it hard to breathe. He didn't have a sister. Not now. When Beverly had been alive, though, he hadn't really appreciated her. What he wouldn't give to have that time back so he could redo it, make it right, so he could love her as

Elizabeth obviously loved her sister. He pushed the thought away.

"If I had one, and she was twenty-eight, I'd figure she's old enough to know what she's doing."

Her expression softened. "I should, too, I guess, but April's not…a responsible twenty-eight."

"Who *is* in their twenties? Thirty-something maybe…forty-something probably, but twenty?" He shook his head. "I don't think so."

She bristled. "I'm twenty-eight and I'm certainly responsible."

He sent her a measuring stare and silently agreed. There were shadows in those beautiful dark eyes and a tenseness in her face he hadn't noticed before. Hell, she'd probably been responsible when she was eight, much less twenty-eight. Why? What demons did she have no one else knew about?

"I can see that," he said finally. "It's obvious or you wouldn't be worried about…" He waited for her to supply the name.

"April," she said reluctantly. "April Benoit. And I'm Elizabeth."

"I'm John Mallory."

With the exchange of names, her attitude shifted and became even more remote. A thick silence grew between them, then she broke it by speaking stiffly. "I'm sorry, Detective Mallory, to dump all this on you. The strain's getting to me, I guess. Believe me,

I usually don't tell strangers intimate details of my life like this.''

"It's John,'' he said, ''and don't worry about it. I'd be happy to look into it for you.''

Her eyes widened in surprise. ''Oh, no. Please. That's not why I was telling you.''

"I know that,'' he said. ''But I don't mind. It'd be easy for me. I can check some things Missing Persons might not get around to so fast.'' *If ever.*

"I appreciate it, but…'' Rising from the bench, she ran a hand over her jacket, a reassuring move as if checking her defensive shell. ''I really can't ask you to do that.''

John stood, too. He was a tall man, an inch over six feet. When he looked in her eyes, they weren't that far beneath his own. ''You're not asking. I'm offering.''

Her expression closed, but not before he saw a glimpse of how she really felt. She wanted his assistance, wanted it desperately, but for some reason, couldn't allow herself to accept it.

"No.'' Her voice was firm now. ''I can't let you do that.''

His curiosity got the better of him, and he pushed, more than he usually did. ''I'm offering you some help. Why don't you want it?''

She blinked at his bluntness, a sweep of dark lashes falling over her eyes before she looked at him again. ''April will turn up sooner or later,'' she said in a stilted voice. "It's not that I don't appreciate your offer, but I don't want to pull you into our personal problems. I can handle it by myself. I always have."

Something in the way she spoke took his curiosity to another level, it raised his antennae. His cop antennae. "You have some personal problems?"

Her gaze didn't waver. "Doesn't everyone?"

He didn't answer, but let the silence build. Most people felt uncomfortable with the quiet. He found out all kinds of interesting things when they started to talk to fill the void. Elizabeth Benoit simply stared at him.

"Then she's not in any kind of trouble?"

She hesitated only a second, no more. "Not that I'm aware of."

They stared at each other a moment longer, then she extended her hand. "Thank you for listening to me, Mr. Mallory. I won't bother you again."

He took her fingers in his, the touch impersonal, the message clear. "I hope things work out," he said, his voice equally neutral.

They shook hands, then Elizabeth turned and walked away. John watched her until she disappeared around the corner.

SHE COULDN'T get him out of her mind.

The following morning, as Elizabeth sat at her desk and stared out the window, all she could think about was John Mallory's offer. God, it'd been hard to turn him down! She'd wanted so badly to accept his help, but it'd been so long since she'd trusted anyone she'd said no without even thinking. He'd looked at her with such sympathy, though, such patience. Something in his gaze had made her *want* to trust him. Maybe because he'd listened to her story without even blinking. Of course, he *was* a cop and that did make a difference, she supposed. She shook her head in disbelief. How long had it been since she'd let anyone see her cry? Since she'd cried, period?

Had she lost her mind?

She focused on the traffic outside her window. It was as snarled and tangled as her nerves, but she knew one thing for certain. No one ever got a free ride. No one. People—men, especially—didn't offer their help without expecting something in return. She'd been on her own, taking care of April and her mother, since she was twelve years old, and if she hadn't learned that particular lesson, she'd learned nothing at all.

Why did he want to help her, anyway? Was he simply that nice? Was anyone?

Just the previous week she'd seen John and a little girl—his daughter, she presumed—crossing the street out front. He'd had the child's hand in his, and they were obviously going to the park. Elizabeth had watched them from her living-room window, a lump forming in her throat as she'd remembered holding her own father's hand. Until his death, she'd thought he'd hung the moon and the stars, as well. Everything he did was perfect. He'd supported them all, Elizabeth, April and their mother, in high style, and he'd seemed to be the most loving, wonderful man on earth. The best father a child could possibly want. A faultless husband, too. Until things had changed.

Her intercom buzzed, and she answered, her eyes focused on the window and the traffic below, her mind focused on her father and the child she'd been.

"Linda Tremont is here." Betty sounded worried, and Elizabeth tensed. Her secretary was usually unflappable. "She doesn't have an appointment and I tried to get her to wait, but she's insisting." Betty lowered her voice. "She seems quite upset. Can you see her?"

Elizabeth held back a groan. She didn't want to deal with this now, not with April on her mind, but she couldn't put it off forever. "Send her in."

A second later the door opened. As Linda Tremont crossed the carpeted expanse between the door and her mahogany desk, Elizabeth noticed that the woman seemed to have aged ten years since the first time they'd met. Behind the glasses she wore there were puffy circles of worry under her eyes, and her mouth was a thin line of tension. Even her posture was stiff and anxious.

She perched nervously on the edge of one of the pair of wingback chairs in front of the desk. "Have you finished the report yet? I need to know," she said without preamble. "I heard from another investor this week who's very worried. Word's getting out that Tony's being investigated—"

"Mrs. Tremont—"

"Call me Linda," she broke in, her voice rising slightly. "I prefer anyone who gives me bad news to at least use my first name."

Linda looked as if she might shatter, and Elizabeth gazed at her with compassion. She liked her and could certainly understand her worry.

"I haven't finished my report yet," Elizabeth said gently. "I've done some preliminary work, but I can't give you any details, and I'm sure you understand why."

"But you contacted me! Why can't you tell me more?"

"I had to talk to you in order to obtain your records, and you've been very cooperative, which I appreciate. But I can't get into the facts of the case with you, Linda, I'm sorry. That's just not how I work."

"Don't give me the specifics, then," she urged. "But please…I need to know for my clients' sake as much as for my own. Is…is Tony in trouble?"

Elizabeth sipped from a glass of water on her desk, trying to buy time and figure out how to say what Linda needed to hear without giving away too much. She had to be very careful. She chose her words with precision. "Are you familiar with the term *churning?*"

"Of course I am. That's when brokers have their clients buy and sell stock just to generate more commissions for themselves." Her eyes grew large. "Are you saying Tony's been churning accounts?"

Elizabeth kept quiet. S.E.C. investigations were not secret affairs; they couldn't be because of their complex nature and the longevity of the task, but Elizabeth had her own set of rules. She'd already said more than she usually did.

Taking Elizabeth's silence for the answer it was, Linda Tremont removed her glasses and pinched the bridge of her nose. "How much?" She didn't look up.

"I'm not at liberty to say."

Linda Tremont's voice went up. "Thousands? Millions? Can't you give me some idea?"

Elizabeth glanced down at her desk, then up again. "If churning *were* involved, and I'm not saying it is, then I'd point to the latter figure as more accurate than the former."

Linda gasped. "My God! I...I can't believe this!"

Again Elizabeth stayed silent. She liked to be more certain when it came to figures, which her superiors at the S.E.C. appreciated. She'd given them some details about the investigation, but not enough for them to start legal action. Yet. She wanted to be absolutely confident that was necessary, and while she had a strong suspicion it was, for her own peace of mind, she needed just a little more.

The older woman slumped back into the chair, almost shrinking before Elizabeth's eyes. "I was afraid it wasn't good, but millions...."

"I'm not finished yet, Linda. Don't jump to any conclusions before the report is final."

Linda looked up, her expression so bleak Elizabeth almost couldn't bear to finish what she was going to say. "When I'm done, the total will be more accurate."

She suddenly wished she'd skipped that extra cup of coffee. Her stomach felt as if it wanted to rebel.

"What's he going to do?" Linda Tremont looked even more defenseless and uncertain without her glasses. "He's my baby brother...."

Elizabeth had met Tony Masterson twice while gathering information. In his early thirties, he had the polished sophisticated look of a man you could trust. She could see how blue-haired ladies would have been happy to hand over their money to him. He'd assured Elizabeth that nothing was wrong, and if any irregularities were found, his underlings would know more about it than he would.

Linda had told Elizabeth a little about him, nervously, during one of their meetings. Almost apologetically she'd explained that he'd played tournament bridge all through college, and when he'd graduated with a business degree, he'd used the contacts of his bridge players and fraternity brothers to lead them and their elderly relatives straight into his family's financial-planning company, Masterson Investments. Where he'd promptly begun to take advantage of them, Elizabeth had since realized.

"I need to set up another meeting with Tony to go over some points. Is he around?"

Linda's lips tightened. "He's in Europe this week, but he'll be back on Friday. He's speaking at a conference." She paused. "Have you contacted the S.E.C.?"

"I haven't given them a final report since I'm not done yet. Once I finish and send them everything, they'll start an official investigation and assign one of their own attorneys to go over everything."

Elizabeth didn't generally offer advice, but the empathy she felt for Linda Tremont made her want to help. Putting her elbows on the desk, Elizabeth leaned closer. "If I were you, I'd get a good lawyer, Linda. Leo Stevens is excellent. He's with Baker and Tornago." The woman on the other side of the desk was so pale she looked as if she might faint. "Would you like me to call him for you?" Elizabeth asked softly. "I'd be happy to introduce you—"

"No!" Linda shook her head, almost violently,

then seemed to realize what she was doing and stopped. "I...I'll call him, myself. I...I appreciate the offer, but I have to take care of this on my own. I'm sure you understand."

"Of course."

"When will you finish the report?"

"Within the next two weeks. I've been working on it mostly at home. I can concentrate better there."

Linda rose painfully and walked to the door. Then she turned and asked, "Is there any way you could, well, finish it sooner? The longer it goes on, the worse it will be. For everyone."

Elizabeth hesitated. With April's disappearance, she couldn't get her regular work done, much less hurry things up.

"I wouldn't ask if it wasn't so important."

"It's not that," Elizabeth answered finally. "I...I have some family problems of my own right now that I'm trying to deal with, that's all."

"I'm sorry. Nothing too serious, I hope." Linda stood by the door expectantly, obviously waiting for more.

"My sister's missing," Elizabeth said bluntly. "We met for our birthday dinner Sunday, then the next morning she was gone. Along with my car. I haven't seen her since."

A disconcerting silence fell between the two women before Linda spoke awkwardly. "I'm so sorry. You don't have any idea where she might be?''

"Not really. I've called the police and reported it. That's all I can do.''

The expression on Linda's face shifted. It held something Elizabeth couldn't read, but whatever it was it contained more than a hint of disapproval. "You called the police?'' she echoed.

"Yes, and I filed a missing person's report. It's all I can do.''

"Of course. But try not to worry. I'm sure she'll turn up.'' She paused. Then said, "Just let me know about the report as soon as you can.'' With that Linda Tremont left, closing the door softly behind her.

Try not to worry? What kind of advice was that? How could you not worry if your sister had disappeared—even if she *had* done it before.

Elizabeth swung her chair around and looked out the office window, her mind going right back to the subject it'd been on before. John Mallory. Brown eyes, a strong jaw and a tough lean body that looked as though it could hold its own in any battle.

She'd seen him before. When April was visiting one day, she'd asked Elizabeth who the "cowboy" was in the unit at the end. Elizabeth had glanced out her window and recognized his white starched shirt, the snug jeans, the heeled boots. A lot of men in Texas dressed that way—it was almost a uniform—but on John, the clothes looked just right. For some perverse reason, Elizabeth had pretended not to know who April was asking about.

But Elizabeth had known all right, had surprisingly even found herself curious about the tall man in the polished boots. Usually she didn't notice men. She'd had one serious relationship since she'd left college, but it hadn't worked out. She'd dated another attorney, Jack Montgomery, for almost six months. He'd wanted a home with a wife who stayed in it, and Elizabeth couldn't do that. She wasn't wife and mother material. She'd told him so and he'd never called again.

That was part of the reason she'd turned down John's help. Slipping up and pouring out her personal problems was one thing—a mistake, sure, but not unrecoverable. Any more contact might lead to something else, though, and she wasn't interested in that. Not now.

IT WAS AFTER SIX when John pushed open the heavy glass door of the high rise that housed Benoit Consulting. He wasn't really prepared for it to open, but it did, gliding soundlessly outward. He knew Elizabeth worked late most nights—at home her lights never came on before seven or sometimes eight— but he hadn't really thought the whole building would be open at this hour. A dark-haired Hispanic woman looked up as he entered. To get past her, an electronic card reader on the wall had to first be satisfied. Apparently there were a lot of private consultants in the complex, sharing facilities.

"May I help you?" she asked pleasantly.

He skipped the badge routine and just smiled. "I'm a friend of Elizabeth Benoit's, Benoit Consulting. Is she still around by any chance?"

"I'll check."

A moment later the receptionist hung up the phone, shaking her head. "I'm sorry, sir, but it appears as if Ms. Benoit's office is closed. No one is answering." The woman frowned, then snapped her fingers. "She might be in the gym downstairs, working out. Someone will have to buzz you in, but you could try there."

"Great, thanks." He turned and left, the plush carpeting swallowing the sound of his footsteps.

As he waited for the elevator, John wondered just what in the hell he was doing there, anyway. When he'd picked up the phone at his desk earlier that day to call information for Elizabeth's work number, he'd half hoped they wouldn't have a listing. They did, however, and then he'd called the number to get the address. He didn't know exactly what she did, but she had the look of someone who would want columns to add up properly. Putting the matter aside, he'd worked a little longer, then headed home for a quick bite, intending to return to the station. Marsha had succeeded in screwing up his time with

Lisa, after all, so he'd decided to work all evening and catch up on the mountain of papers hiding his desk. It'd tame his anger a bit. Somewhere between Central and his place, though, he'd aimed the truck west.

And here he was.

The elevator dinged, the doors opened and he walked out. For whatever reason, Elizabeth had made it more than clear she didn't want his help, even though, he sensed, she really wanted it.

Turning a corner in the basement a few minutes later, John found the gym. He'd been in executive workout clubs before and knew what to expect. White carpet, polished chrome, a juice bar in one corner. There was usually a babe at the front desk who knocked your eyes to the back of your head, too. A man in a navy warm-up suit exited just as John approached, holding the door open for him. John nodded his thanks and entered. Not what he'd expected.

The gym was one large bare room with a concrete floor and mirrors lining the walls. Four or five people were using the various machines and free weights. John's gaze swept the room until he saw Elizabeth. She was stretched out on a climbing machine, her arms straining high above her head, her legs—her very long legs—pumping beneath her.

He watched her for a moment. She didn't have on fancy workout gear or two-hundred-dollar running shoes. She wore sneakers that were scuffed and well-worn, an old pair of black shorts and a ragged T-shirt with missing arms, leaving gaping holes. Beneath the cut-outs, he could see the outline of a no-nonsense jogging bra. A faded sweatband was pushed up on her forehead, holding back the straggling strands of hair that had escaped the rubber band at the back.

She was the sexiest woman in the room.

Their gazes collided in the mirror, and he watched her expression go from blank to annoyed. She obviously wasn't happy to see him. She stepped off the machine, grabbed her towel and crossed to him.

"Detective Mallory. Are you here to see me or did you come to join our club?"

He looked around a bit before meeting her gaze again. He needed the extra time to get his pulse back to where it belonged, preferably somewhere below 150. Beneath those suits she wore, she had a body that matched her legs. He took a deep breath, focused on her eyes and smiled easily.

"I don't think so," he said. "It's not much better than the police gym."

"The building owner spends his money where it shows—in the offices." She shrugged. "It doesn't matter. This gets the job done."

"I can see that."

She didn't react to what he'd said, though he

could tell his compliment had registered. Apparently, she didn't know how to respond. "How did you find me?"

"There was no one in your office. The receptionist told me you might be down here."

"And how did you know where I worked?"

She was a careful one, that was for sure. He held out his hands palms up—a gesture meant to show no threat. "I'm a cop, remember? It's my job to find out things." He smiled. "Actually I noticed the report you had in your hands when we were talking at the mailboxes. It had the name of your company on it."

She seemed to relax just a fraction, but the watchful air didn't leave her. She reminded him of a cat that used to hang around the station. Sleek black hair, cagey eyes, a tense body that always looked as if it was about to spring the other way.

For a long moment they looked at each other, then suddenly her wariness changed to fear, her fingers going to her throat. "Oh, God—this isn't about April, is it? You aren't here to tell me they found her...her body or anything?"

He felt a rush of empathy and shook his head immediately. "No, no. She hasn't been found, nothing like that."

She exhaled and visibly relaxed.

"The reason I'm here *is* your sister, though."

The guarded look came back.

"I did a little checking after we spoke—"

"After I told you your help wasn't necessary?"

He inclined his head, an admission of guilt. "Yes. After that."

If he expected angry words, he was disappointed. She simply looked at him with a level gaze he couldn't read. "And?"

He looked directly into her bottomless eyes and said, "I couldn't help but wonder—why didn't you tell me your sister's a stripper?"

CHAPTER THREE

ELIZABETH COULD feel the color start at her throat and work its way upward, until her face flushed a deep hot red.

"I don't care for that word," she answered tightly. "She's a dancer, an exotic dancer. And I don't see what business it is of yours, one way or the other. I called the police again this morning, and the *proper* people are working on the case."

"I didn't mean to insult you."

"You didn't insult me, but I have a problem with dancers being called strippers. One inaccurate word generally leads to another, and in this case it's usually *hooker.*"

"*Is* she a hooker?"

Elizabeth drew in a sharp disbelieving breath. Without another word, she whirled and headed for the door to the showers, her sneakers slapping angrily on the floor. Before she could reach it, he was standing in front of her. He put a hand on her arm, stopping her.

She looked down at his fingers, then back up at

him. "Take your hand off me and please leave. Now."

"I'm only trying to help you," he said quietly.

He was wearing the same look of compassion he'd had when he'd met her at the mailboxes, and something inside of her melted. But she reminded herself of her thoughts only a few hours before, and refused to give in. "That's supposed to help me? Calling my sister a hooker?"

"I didn't *call* her that," he said evenly. "I asked you if she *was* one. It could play in why she'd disappeared."

Elizabeth stared at him, her jaw clenched, her hands in two fists at her side. "My sister dances for a living. It isn't a great business to be in and I wish she'd find another career, but I don't appreciate your question."

His deep brown eyes held hers. "I'm sorry. Like I said, I didn't mean to insult you...or her."

She didn't answer, *couldn't* answer. When he spoke, his voice was even softer than before. The low timbre of it caused a shiver to travel up her arms and down her back. "Look, I may not always be tactful, but if you want to find your sister, I can help. I'm an honest cop and you can trust me."

"I've heard those words before."

"Not from me, you haven't."

She didn't want to acknowledge it, but something—a quick dash of intuition?—flickered inside her. She told herself she just *wanted* to believe him, so that's what was happening, but in his gaze was something awfully close to sincerity.

Would it be so terrible to let him help her?

He read her hesitation. "Why don't you get dressed? I'll wait for you, then we'll hit the deli on the corner and talk. You haven't eaten dinner, have you?"

"No, but—"

"Get your clothes on," he said gently but insistently. "I want to talk to you some more and I have to go back to work in an hour. I was on my way home to grab something for dinner and swung by here, instead. I can't face Central on an empty stomach." When she didn't answer, he spoke again, his eyes warming as they narrowed and crinkled at the corners. "C'mon—it's just a sandwich, not a lifetime commitment."

She looked into his eyes. "All right," she said finally. "But it'll take me a few minutes to get dressed."

"I can wait. I'm a patient man."

She turned and went into the locker room. Showering and dressing quickly, she found herself in front of the mirror, taking a little more care than usual with her makeup. When she realized what she was doing, she tossed the tube of mascara into her purse and snapped it shut. Two minutes later she was walking out the door with John at her side.

Alarms were going off in her head, but she ignored them.

As they made their way to the tiny deli, dusk was starting to fall and the summer heat hadn't relented a bit. Traffic was steady, too, and the diesel and gasoline fumes only added to the humidity. Elizabeth was happy to enter the frigid air-conditioning of the restaurant. The place was empty of customers, six forlorn booths lining the wall, three tables on the other side. They took the last booth, and the teenager who came for their order looked as if she'd rather be anywhere but standing by the red-checked tablecloth. She disappeared into the back and returned promptly with the coffee they'd wanted, promising their sandwiches would be ready shortly. As soon as she left, John began to speak, picking up exactly where they'd left off.

"I don't care what your sister does for a living, and I wasn't trying to imply anything. The only reason I said what I did about her occupation was that it's not exactly like being a school teacher. The people who run those clubs are a pretty tough bunch."

"I know." Elizabeth sighed. "I've been trying to get her to quit."

"But the money's good."

"The money's great for someone who never finished college and has no other skills. She doesn't really have another choice right now."

"Even though you've offered to help."

It wasn't a question. He said the words as if he knew them to be true. "I have," she answered, anyway. "I've offered to do everything...anything. But April can be stubborn. Even when she was a little kid and we were really close, she wanted to be herself, completely apart from me. She went nuts if Mom tried to dress us alike."

"That's understandable."

"What do you mean?" Elizabeth frowned. "A lot of twins dress the same."

"And it always invites comparisons, doesn't it?"

She nodded.

"Who in their right mind would want to be compared to you?" he said softly.

Over the table, his gaze locked with hers before she quickly looked away, the offhand compliment completely disarming her. She picked up her coffee and took a sip, then said, "When we were younger, we looked exactly alike, but now she's blond and thinner and—"

"She colors her hair?"

"Yes, perms it, too, and it's also longer than mine. She wears green contacts, as well."

"To make the differences even greater?"

Elizabeth answered reluctantly. "I never thought of it that way, but yes, maybe so."

He nodded and took a swallow of coffee.

"How did you find out?" she asked. "I mean, that April danced?"

"You mentioned her address when we spoke."

She waited for more. When it didn't come, she asked, "And? Did you talk to her neighbors or something?"

He smiled then, the corners of his full lips going up and pulling her gaze. Distracting her, even.

"I can't be giving all my detective secrets away, now can I?" He arched one eyebrow, obviously prepared to say nothing more.

"Have you been to the club where she works?"

"Not yet. I was going to do that tomorrow. Is she still at the Esquire?"

Elizabeth nodded. What John didn't know, he found out quickly enough, it seemed. "She's been there about three years. Ever since we moved here." She paused to gather her thoughts, then spoke quickly before she changed her mind, telling him about the conversation with Greg Lansing.

"What kind of trouble do you think he was talking about?"

"I have no idea." She caught his look. "And before you ask, April is *not* into drugs. She won't even take an aspirin when she has a headache."

"Did she owe people money?"

Elizabeth laughed, a sound without humor. "Only me. She's very generous with all her friends. If they need anything, they know they can come to her...and if she doesn't have it, she usually comes to me."

"Does she have any enemies?"

Elizabeth spoke reluctantly. "There is this woman...one of the other dancers. Her name is Tracy Kensington. She hates April even though April's tried to be friends with her. Tracy was the top dancer at the club before April got there. Her tips went way down once the men saw April."

He nodded without changing his expression, his next question throwing her off completely. "Where'd you say you lived before?"

The voice was still friendly and open, but for the first time, Elizabeth heard an edge beneath all the questions, an edge that reminded her of what he was. A Houston cop.

"Dallas," she answered cautiously. What could he do with that tidbit of information?

"Did she dance there?"

"Yes."

"Where?"

Elizabeth's mouth turned dry, a lump the size of a baseball lodging in the deepest part of her throat. "At a place called the Yellow Rose."

"How long was she there?"

"Years. We were going to college in Dallas and that's when...when she started."

His gaze narrowed, and she grew warm, the neckline of her blouse suddenly choking her. She tugged at the collar. God, she thought, all he had to do was ask her and she'd tell him. Everything. She closed her eyes for a second, the room spinning behind her lids. Taking a deep breath, she forced her eyes open and tried her best to look normal. The waitress saved the day by appearing with their sandwiches.

He noticed, anyway. "You okay?" he asked as soon as the teenager left.

"I...I'm fine," she lied. "It's just that I can't quite believe April's still gone. I can't think about anything but her, yet I have piles of work waiting and a rush job to boot."

"What exactly do you do up there in that big fancy office?"

Grateful he'd switched the subject, she used her cocktail-party version to explain what she did. He asked all the right questions, though, even seemed interested. She soon found herself telling him about the Masterson case in detail.

John shook his head. "Amazing. Here's a guy who's got all the advantages in the world—money, power—and he still feels compelled to go out and rob people. Makes you wonder, doesn't it?"

She pulled a paper napkin from the container on the table and dabbed her mouth. "Not really. There's always someone waiting to take advantage of people who can't take care of themselves."

They talked for another few minutes, then John called for the bill, which, despite her protests, he insisted on paying. Within minutes of stepping back into the humid Houston air, Elizabeth's blouse was clinging to her back and a damp curl of hair had wound itself around her neck. While they'd been eating, enormous black thunderclouds had moved in and looked ready to burst any moment. The wind picked up and sent an empty pop can rattling along the gutter.

They hurried to Elizabeth's office building. When they reached the main door, the rain still hadn't started. John put a hand on Elizabeth's arm to stop her from going in. She looked at him expectantly. He was tall enough that she had to tilt her head slightly to see him as he spoke.

"Listen, Elizabeth, I won't do anything else unless you want me to." She could read the sincerity in his eyes, hear it in his voice. "Where we take this now is entirely up to you."

Thunder rumbled above their heads, and Elizabeth felt an echoing sensation in her body. She didn't know what she should do. "I...I don't want you to go to any trouble. I'm sure you have enough work of your own, and—"

He interrupted her. "I don't have time for anything but the truth, so just say what you want to, Elizabeth. You don't trust me. You can't figure out why I'd want to help you when we're basically strangers. Am I right?"

His words forced her to face facts. "Yes," she said, "I *don't* trust you. But it's not personal. It's just the way I am. The way I...turned out."

"And there's nothing wrong with that," he answered, surprising her once again. "Women need to be careful these days. Hell, we *all* need to be careful. Like you said before, there're a lot of sharks out there." He paused, then, "But I'm a cop. I like to put the pieces of the puzzle together and make sense of it when it doesn't look as if there's any sense left. And I like to help people." He held his hands out again, a gesture he tended to use frequently, she noted. "That's it, pure and simple. I don't have any ulterior motive."

She looked into his warm brown eyes and didn't believe a word he said. He *did* have a motive; everyone had one for everything they did, whether they knew it or not. The only question was if his was good or bad.

"I know you're worried and I know you want your sister back. I understand that better than you think I do, believe me." He reached out and touched her arm again briefly, as if to confirm his words. The gesture was warm and somehow reassuring. It scared her, but she believed him. "If you do this on your own, though, you may never find out what happened to her—until her body turns up."

Elizabeth's heart clutched. "Do you think she's dead?"

"I don't know, but unless I start to look, we may never know."

Still she hesitated, torn with indecision. Should

she trust him and allow herself to be indebted to him? Then she wondered why she was even debating the issue—she'd known the outcome when she'd started answering his questions, hadn't she? This might finally be one of those things she couldn't handle on her own. Her brain was screaming, though. *Don't trust him. He can hurt you. You like him too much already.*

"If I don't get involved," he went on, "Missing Persons will do nothing." His voice held regret. "I'm sorry, but the reality is they're not going to get excited about this, Elizabeth. Not for someone in April's position."

She studied his face and read the truth, as painful as it was, in his eyes. He was right, she thought, her chest tightening as she remembered the woman she'd reported April's disappearance to. Tuesday morning, Elizabeth had called her back and requested an official investigation, but she knew that route would bring nothing. The woman had taken the information, then quickly transferred her to the stolen car division. When she'd explained her sister had probably taken her car, they were even less interested than the previous department. And what about her own efforts? In the four days since April had been gone, Elizabeth had called the club, talked to April's neighbors, her landlord and everyone else she could possibly think of, and they'd been no help at all. She'd even put up posters around the apartment building, but not a single call had come in. Did she have any other choice but depending on this man?

She nodded and said slowly, "Well, I guess it wouldn't hurt if you just ask a few questions."

As soon as the words were out, Elizabeth wanted to take them back. What kind of terrible mistake was she making?

He met her eyes. "I'll do the best I can, Elizabeth. And you won't regret letting me help, I promise."

FRIDAY EVENING John pulled up to the curb and parked his car, staring over the steering wheel at the house where he used to live. The red brick glowed dully in the late-evening light, and he could see the azaleas had just been trimmed. The home was in a nice neighborhood, more expensive than he'd liked, but Marsha had insisted, saying her salary would make up the difference they needed. Now she lived there by herself—her and Lisa. And Marsha's father gave her all the money she wanted—since John was no longer there to protest.

He'd fully intended to be here yesterday, but Marsha had called him that morning and put Lisa on the line. Her mother hadn't changed a thing, and she'd been jumping with enthusiasm for her scheduled haircut. He hadn't had the heart to insist she see him, instead. Dinner in the cafeteria and the bunk bed in his apartment didn't hold the same appeal as a fancy beauty salon did to a little girl. Gritting his teeth, he'd simply given in to Marsha, deciding on his own to stop by this evening. It'd given him the time to catch Elizabeth at her office, but he hadn't liked the situation. He wasn't going to let two weeks pass without seeing his daughter.

His eyes went to the upstairs corner bedroom—Lisa's room. A small lamp shone in front of the window. It was her Goofy lamp. She loved the damn thing. He'd got it for her last year when they'd taken a trip to Disneyland. For one whole week, he'd had her all to himself, and more than once the thought of never coming back had crossed his mind. He was a cop—he knew how to disappear—and the temptation had been awfully strong to take his daughter, find a quiet little town in California, change his name and start a new life. In the end he'd resisted, of course. Not because he didn't want to hurt Marsha, not even because it was against the law, but because Lisa deserved better. She had the right to a father *and* a mother, regardless of how selfish and egocentric the mother happened to be.

He got out of the car and started up the sidewalk, his thoughts turning to the woman he'd had dinner with the night before. He'd put Elizabeth Benoit into the same mold as Marsha, and he hadn't even known her. Just because the two women were beautiful, he'd assumed Elizabeth was as self-centered as his ex. A stupid premise, he realized now. Still, he'd known other beautiful women who definitely thought the sun revolved around themselves, and to guess Elizabeth was the same hadn't really been that far out of line.

He'd been wrong, though. Very wrong.

Knocking on the door and waiting for it to open, he thought back to the conversation at the deli. Elizabeth Benoit loved her sister, loved her and wanted her back, no matter what. Despite her innate mistrust, she'd realized she'd needed his help. He wondered once more about the pain he sometimes saw in those eyes. Who had hurt her so badly? Why hadn't she ever married?

The doorknob turned and John smiled. Lisa always answered it when he was expected. But Lisa wasn't standing there when the door opened. Marsha was.

She looked surprised to see him, and for a moment, he caught a glimpse of the woman he'd once loved. She really was beautiful. "John! What are you doing here?"

"I came to see Lisa. Since yesterday was out, I wanted to visit with her a bit."

"John..." She shook her head and said his name with resignation. Unbelievably, just beneath the surface, he heard a hint of sympathy, then decided he was imagining it. "I *told* you the other day that Lisa had a birthday party to go to this evening. That was why I had to have her hair cut. Weren't you listening?''

He inhaled deeply and let the air out on a sigh. ''Obviously I wasn't.''

''If you'd pay attention when we have a conversation, these things wouldn't happen.''

He couldn't argue with the truth, could he? Especially as he'd been thinking of Elizabeth at the time. ''Then I have to wait until next week?''

Her expression softened minutely. ''We're going to Galveston in the morning,'' she said. ''If you want to come down to the beach house, you could see her there.''

Marsha's father owned a huge beachfront villa, and every weekend in the summer, the whole family met there. ''I don't have the time. It takes two hours to get there when the traffic's bad. And I'm on call this weekend.''

Her bitter tone returned with the mention of his job. She'd never liked his being a cop; it didn't hold enough status, not to mention earn enough money. ''Then I guess you'll just have to wait. And don't blame it on me, either. You have the option.''

Her changed attitude brought back all the wrong memories, and he responded in a voice less than kind. ''All right. But you have her here and ready next Thursday. I don't like going so long without seeing her.''

She gave him a curt nod, and he walked away,

not even bothering to say goodbye. The door slammed behind him before he was even off the porch.

Back in the truck he sat for a moment and fumed. Why go home? He'd just sit there and get madder. He wheeled the vehicle around and headed for the Richmond strip. Within ten minutes he pulled into the parking lot of the Esquire Club.

He found a spot but didn't get out right away, choosing instead to sit for a moment and check out the setup. He wanted to calm down, too. He couldn't work when he was this angry. He'd miss things, important details. He took three deep breaths, then looked out the window at the nightclub.

Stuccoed and well lit, it had the appearance of a home on River Oaks Boulevard. Looking exactly like a miniature Tara, the front stretched at least seventy-five feet with white columns going from one end to the other. A series of regularly spaced windows, wide and arched, lined the wall. Behind them, he could see men and women moving about, as if at a party. The setup looked pretty good, but then these joints usually did—in the dark.

Stepping out of his vehicle, John wove his way through the parking lot, his initial impression of wealth reinforced by the cars he passed. The vehicles were mainly European: BMWs and Mercedes, even a few Rolls-Royces. No good ol' boy pickups here—except for his. Reaching the veranda where scattered groups of men stood, John saw several faces he recognized from the news. Many of the men were smoking cigars, expensive clouds of blue hanging over their heads. Their laughter was full and assured. With a glance he could tell who they were, even the ones he didn't recognize. They were the high-rollers of Houston. Powerful men. Rich men.

John pushed his way through the crowd and into the club where the smells of expensive perfume and call-name liquor hit him hard. People flowed around him in what looked like the entry hall of an elegant home. From somewhere in the rear came the faint strains of music, but certainly not the overwhelming blast that usually assaulted you when you entered a bar. A discreet sign near the door announced a fifty-dollar cover and a two-drink minimum. Before he could decide which role to take—cop or patron—a young woman approached him. Red sheath, high heels, blond hair.

"Welcome to the Esquire Club," she said. "How may I direct you this evening?"

It was a novel approach, he'd give them that.

"What do you feel like tonight?" she prompted when he didn't answer right away. "We have the club divided into different areas depending on your mood. Wild music? Something soothing? A little country or rock and roll?" She smiled seductively, then put her fingertips on his arm. "Name your pleasure, sir. We have them all."

"I'd like to see Mr. Lansing." He spoke politely and made no move to pull out his badge. He didn't have to. For some reason, he felt this one would know the drill.

She blinked, then her expression hardened minutely. "Of course," she answered, her voice still cordial but now lacking the coquettish tone. "Let me see if he's in." She reached for the phone sitting on a nearby desk, but John reached out faster.

Smiling, he stilled her movement. "What do you say we just go to the back? Surprise him?"

"Mr. Lansing doesn't like surprises."

"That's too bad," John said. "Just take me to his office."

She hesitated a second, because there was nothing else she could do. With a curt nod she started toward the rear of the club. John followed, but his steps were slower. He took his time, looking into the separate areas as they passed by.

Different music flowed from each one, matched by the decor. The first resembled a gentleman's study. Padded leather chairs were grouped around square wooden tables, and the air was filled with the same expensive smoke he'd noticed earlier. No doubt imported—and illegal—cigars. He didn't recognize the music, but it was slow and seductive. A woman in a flowing sheer dress was moving dreamily to it on a small stage near the front of the room. Beneath the gauzy fabric, she wore a G-string and nothing more. Some of the men were watching her, but most were talking among themselves, drinks on the tables before them. There were just as many women in the room as men.

The next room thrummed with rock music, and it had the look he'd come to associate with this kind of club. Low lights, a long bar across one wall. The hazy miasma of smoke smelled cheaper here. The walls were painted black and mirrors lined the area behind the bar. Small round tables dotted the floor, just large enough for two drinks and the high heels of the women who would dance on them. It would look garish and shabby in the daylight hours, but at the moment it oozed a kind of erotic appeal, primarily due to the woman in the center of the stage.

She had the body, she had the moves, she had it all. To say she was sexy didn't do the word justice—or her, for that matter. She wasn't wearing much beyond a G-string and heels, and her long red hair flowed over one bare shoulder like silk. She moved in perfect time to the music, an old Santana song he recognized immediately, "Black Magic Woman." As he stared, she caught his gaze and held it.

John was as red-blooded as the next guy, and he felt his body respond automatically. The woman grinned as if sensing his reaction, then she broke the moment, moving sinuously around the pole to the center of the stage. Putting her back to the glowing column made of neon, she bent over to the floor. The red hair followed in a graceful sweep. John stared a few seconds more, then let his interest dissipate. Up there, she was beautiful and sexy, but something told him that, like the room, she might not fare too well in brighter light.

He turned to leave, the waiting blonde watching him with a jaded expression. As he came toward her, she turned and continued to the back of the club. John followed and they passed three other rooms. Rap music, country, then finally, in the last room, a voluptuous belly dancer accompanied by a sitar.

The blonde stopped in front of a paneled door and knocked. Apparently hearing an answer over the music that John didn't, she turned the brass handle, then stepped aside to allow John to enter. She pulled the door closed behind him, and the music was silenced. He found himself in front of a massive oak desk, a man built to match sitting in a leather chair behind it. In one meaty hand, he held a cigarette. His eyes were narrow and hard in the smoke that wafted upwards. His long blond hair was pulled back in a ponytail.

John spoke first. "Greg Lansing?"

The man eyed him. "Who wants to know?"

It sounded like a line from a bad movie. John

pulled out his badge now, flipped it open, then closed it and stuck it back in his pocket. "Detective John Mallory. H.P.D. Homicide."

The cold blue eyes flickered once. "What's the problem, Officer?"

"No problem. Just a few questions about one of your dancers—April Benoit."

"She dead?"

"What makes you ask that?"

The big man shrugged. "You said homicide. And she's been missing."

Without being offered, John took one of the chairs in front of the desk and sat, his jacket opening just enough for Lansing to glimpse his holster. He pulled the lapels closer. "She's not dead that I know of, but I'm looking into her disappearance."

"I don't know anything about it." The answer was surly and impatient. With a quick stabbing motion, Greg Lansing leaned over and extinguished the cigarette in a chipped crystal ashtray. "Look, I've got work to do and even if I didn't, I'm in the dark about April—"

"Let's just save each other some trouble here, Mr. Lansing." John spoke smoothly, no hint of aggression in his voice. "Elizabeth Benoit already told me what you said, and I'm here to find out what kind of trouble April's in. Just give me the details and I'll leave."

"I told the woman all I know."

"Why don't I believe that?"

"I don't know."

John shook his head. "Wrong answer."

Like two alley cats, they glared at each other over the desk—a stalemate, but not really. Lansing didn't appear to be a fool; he couldn't be, not if he was running a club as apparently successful as this one. Bars in Houston with good clientele brought in thousands every night. Hell, maybe tens of thousands. Lansing wouldn't jeopardize his setup by pissing off a cop.

"Tell me," John prompted.

The door to the office opened unexpectedly. Both men stared. The red-haired dancer John had watched stood on the threshold. His impression had been right, he thought cynically. She was beautiful, but he could see her looks had just started to fade. In a few more years, the gleam in her eyes would be harder and the glow of her skin somewhat dimmer. She'd have to move down the strip to less expensive clubs where the women were older and the drinks cheaper.

For the moment, though, she still looked good. Very good, as a matter of fact. John let his eyes take her all in. Red hair framing a face with high cheekbones and a generous mouth. Short terry-cloth robe allowing a full view of long shapely legs.

Lansing introduced her.

"Detective Mallory, Tracy Kensington. Tracy, this is Detective Mallory. H.P.D."

Her expression turned stony, giving John another glimpse of her future. Two lines formed on either side of her mouth. "I knew you were a cop. You got the look."

"Tracy..." Lansing's voice rose in warning.

She held up both hands, the robe gaping slightly to reveal a patch of perfect skin.

"He's here about April."

"Have they found her?" She sounded expectant.

"I don't suppose you know anything about her disappearance, do you?" John said by way of an answer. "I heard you and Miss Benoit weren't exactly close."

"Who told you that?" she asked. Not waiting for him to answer, she spit back, "That sister of hers is—"

"Leave," Lansing interrupted. "You can close the door on your way out."

"But I need to talk—"

"Later."

She sent John one last look, then left, slamming the door.

John turned back to Lansing and raised a single eyebrow.

The manager shrugged his wide shoulders at the unspoken but obvious question. "Professional jealousy, I guess you'd say."

"How intense?"

Lansing shook his head. "Not *that* intense. Tracy wouldn't hurt her. She wouldn't want to risk breaking a nail."

"Are you sure?"

Lansing's eyes grew even colder. "Women are vicious creatures, Detective. I wouldn't guarantee anything when it comes to them." He stood up behind the desk. "I hate to be rude, but I've got a club to run, so if there's nothing else…"

John made no move to get up. "Then tell me about April's trouble and I'll be on my way."

"April Benoit's biggest trouble is April Benoit. She gives everyone here a hard time, from the bar girls to Tracy. She's got an attitude, that's the best I can say. A chip on her shoulder."

"But it didn't bother you?"

Greg Lansing's eyes were guarded when they met John's. "What do you mean?"

"You bailed her out of jail a few months ago. Drunk and disorderly." John had run her name the day after he'd spoken with Elizabeth. It was how he'd obtained April's address and place of employment—along with an arrest record Elizabeth obviously didn't know about.

He shrugged. "It wasn't anything. The girls were having a party. One of 'em roped some poor sucker into marrying her, so they were celebrating. They got loud and out of hand. No big deal. April didn't want her sister to know, so I helped her."

"Tell me more."

"There's nothing more to tell."

"Is she beautiful?"

"She knocked Tracy off her pedestal. What does that say?"

"Did she know how to use it?"

Lansing spoke reluctantly. "She can shine on the clients, if that's what you're asking. Every man in the audience thinks she's dancing just for him— more than one always trying to make the promise real."

"Anyone in particular? Was she going out with any of the customers?"

"That's not something we encourage, but the girls don't always listen. She coulda been." He came from behind the desk, his fingers beating an impatient rap against the wood. "I'm sorry, Detective, but I really need to get out there. On the floor. We've got a convention of computer salesmen coming in at ten."

John rose slowly. They were almost eye to eye. "You never defined that trouble for me, Mr. Lansing. The trouble you told Elizabeth about."

Lansing stiffened. "Is this an official investigation?"

"It's as official as it needs to be."

"I don't see a warrant."

"That's 'cause I don't have one." John smiled amicably. "But you know what? I don't need one to make your life miserable, do I? I can call the liquor board, the restaurant inspectors, the SOB people." He waved his hand to the hallway outside. "You know how crazy those sexually oriented businesspeople are. They'd love to see the inside of this place, I'm sure."

The man beside the desk didn't blink.

John pulled one of his business cards from his pocket and flipped it onto the desk. "Give me a call if you think of anything else. I'm sure you want to be as helpful as you can."

Turning, John left the office and started back down the darkened hall. Just as he reached the first room, a slim arm reached out and stopped him. It belonged to Tracy Kensington.

"He didn't tell you anything, did he?"

John looked down at her. "You think you know more?"

"I *know* I know more," she said. Her eyes positively gleamed. "And I also know why Greg's acting like he doesn't."

CHAPTER FOUR

JOHN LOOKED DOWN into the dancer's face. A new song was blaring from one of the rooms, something hard and fast with indecipherable lyrics. In the smoky dark with the weird music playing, her beauty seemed to shift again, and once more, John thought he could see what lay ahead for her.

"Tell me more," he said.

She shook her head. "Oh, no. It's not gonna be that easy, Detective. I know all about this game. You wanna play, you gotta pay."

"What's the price?"

"The going rate," she answered. "And not here, either." She pulled a piece of paper from the pocket of the robe. "Here's my number at home. Call me there. We'll set up a time."

He reached out, but she held on to the card. They stood for a second, connected by the rectangle of cardboard, each holding on to one end. "You're a good-looking man," she said appraisingly. "You available?"

Last week if someone as sexy as Tracy Kensington had asked him this, they'd already be walking out the door together. But for some reason he hesitated, the elusive image of Elizabeth Benoit wavering in the smoky hallway between himself and the half-naked redhead.

He blinked and the mirage disappeared. "Depends," he replied.

"On what?"

"The woman who's asking."

She grinned wolfishly, tilted her head and released the paper. "Give me a call, Detective. I'll make it worth your time."

As ELIZABETH crossed the underground parking garage heading for the car she'd rented, her heels rang eerily on the damp concrete floor, but she paid no attention. Her mind was totally occupied with the useless follow-up call she'd just made to Missing Persons. They knew nothing and were "still working the case." It was Wednesday; April had been gone for a week and a half, and they had done absolutely zip.

She continued toward her car, one step away from screaming out loud. How much longer could she take this limbo? This not knowing?

April, where are you?

She heard a noise behind her and jumped. A car door slamming? Someone dropping something? She looked over her shoulder and peered into the dim corners of the garage but saw nothing. Her heart took an uneasy bump, then she turned around and continued on to her car. She must be going nuts.

The heavy traffic didn't help, and by the time she got home, she felt as if every nerve ending in her body was exposed. Hot and sticky, she changed from her suit to a pair of shorts and a T-shirt. She'd just poured herself a glass of wine when the doorbell rang. Setting the glass down, she went to answer it.

John Mallory stood on the threshold. He looked crisp and clean and cool, his jeans pressed, his white shirt almost glowing in the evening sun. From beneath a pale straw cowboy hat, he smiled, and she felt a warm sensation begin in her chest and spread to the rest of her body.

"I saw you come home." He studied her face. "Could I come in a minute? I need to ask you something."

"S-sure," she stuttered, her reaction to his appearance surprising her. "Please, come in. Would you like a glass of wine? I just poured one for myself."

"That sounds great."

She went into the kitchen and told herself to relax. The advice was followed until she returned to the living room with the two wineglasses and saw John standing by the fireplace looking at a photo of her and April taken just before their twelfth birthday. Dressed for *Swan Lake,* they were posing on the stage of the dance school they'd attended. A sign at their feet proclaimed the name. Harriet Beecham Center for the Performing Arts in Dallas.

He looked up as she entered, inclining his head in the direction of the snapshot. She held her breath, waiting for the inevitable.

"I didn't realize you danced, too." His voice was an inquisitive drawl, innocent and disarming.

"That was a long time ago," she answered quickly, handing him one of the glasses. She tried to divert him. "You said you wanted to ask me something?"

He took the glass, his eyes meeting hers for one long second. She sensed he knew what she was doing, but when he answered her, she gave an inward sigh of relief. He wasn't going to pursue the issue. Just yet.

"Yeah, I did. I went to the club last Friday. Met Tracy and Greg. Nice folks."

She grimaced. "Pretty awful, huh?"

"Tracy told me she knows what happened to April."

Elizabeth's heart skipped a beat, almost stopped in disbelief. "My God! What'd she say?"

"Nothing. She wants me to meet her at her place. Then she wants to be paid for the information."

His words filtered slowly through the drumbeat of her pulse, then Elizabeth shook her head, disappointment swamping her. "She's lying," she said quietly. "She doesn't know anything."

He looked at her with a curious expression. It wasn't surprise—he'd obviously come to a similar conclusion about Tracy himself—but he hadn't expected Elizabeth to do the same. "How do you know that?"

"Well, first off, she hates April's guts. Besides making Tracy's tips dive, Greg dropped her for April, and she's never forgiven him—or April. My sister wanted to be her friend, but Tracy didn't reciprocate. I doubt April would have told her anything really important."

John nodded. "I figured there might be something like that going on. Do you think Tracy would harm April?"

"I don't know," Elizabeth answered. "Tracy's tough. She's been around for a long time and she can hold her own. When Greg told her he wouldn't be dating her anymore, she keyed his 'Vette and put sugar in the tank. One night April came in and caught her cutting up some of her clothes, too. She laughed it off, but I thought it was pretty serious."

"But Tracy's still working there?"

"Did you see her dance?"

"Yeah."

"Then you know why she's still there."

He nodded thoughtfully. "Why else would she be lying? You said 'First off…'"

Elizabeth stared into her wineglass. The pale liquid was sloshing slightly from side to side. She tried to steady her hands, but it was hopeless, so she gave up and raised her face to meet his eyes. "I just meant she might talk with the other girls about it, but not you."

"You know her that well?" His gaze was unwavering.

She swallowed. "We've talked once or twice. I do know her, but my sister and I are very close, and she's talked to me about Tracy. She tells me everything."

"Not exactly. If she told you everything, you'd know where she is."

"You may be right," she admitted. "We have a complicated relationship. It's kinda hard to explain...but she really does tell me a lot, or at least she used to. We had a very close bond, but now...we talk, we spend time together, we *are* close, but not in the way most sisters are. It's genuine, though, I can assure you of that."

He considered her words for a moment, then seemed to accept them and make a decision. "I tell you what—I'm going to have a quick visit with my daughter this evening, but I'd really like to look over April's place. Do you think we could run over there first? It would help me a lot to see how she lived, where she lived..."

When she didn't answer immediately, he spoke again. "You do have a key, don't you?"

"Yes."

"Well, I know it's kinda unexpected, but I might catch something that was missed before."

Elizabeth stalled a second more, a mental image of April's apartment making her cringe. It usually looked as though a tornado had just hit, and that was on the good days. Elizabeth had been over there several times already and had picked up a bit, but her reluctance went deeper than that and she knew it. The Pines was a cheap and ratty complex. April was generous to a fault with money—that's why she never had any—but she preferred to spend it on clothes and on her friends rather than on the place she lived. Elizabeth hated herself for feeling this way, but what kind of impression would John get from her sister's home? Not a good one, she was sure.

She took too long to answer. He read her mind. Again.

"Think I haven't seen messy apartments?" he asked in that soft deceptive voice. "Hell, Elizabeth, remember my job—I go places you couldn't see in your worst nightmares."

"How do you do that?" she said abruptly. "How do you read my mind like that?"

"It's a cop thing," he answered with an easy smile. "We learn it at the academy. Mind Reading 101. Comes right after How to Beat a Suspect."

"Maybe it should come first. Then you wouldn't have to beat them."

He grinned. "Yeah, but where's the fun in that?"

She smiled at the joke, but her expression faded quickly. "If someone has hurt my sister..." She let the words trail off. "Well, let's just say I can understand how you'd be tempted."

Something darkened in his face, a fleeting change she couldn't put words to, but saw nonetheless.

"My job is catching the bad guys," he replied blandly. "I let the courts do the punishing." He picked up his wineglass, drained it, then nodded toward the door. "C'mon, let's go take a look at her place."

JOHN FOLLOWED Elizabeth's car to April's apartment. She'd told him she had some errands to run later, and it'd be easier if they went separately. But that wasn't the real reason she didn't want to ride with him, and John knew it. Elizabeth was one of those people who took every opportunity she could to go it alone. For some reason she felt uncomfortable being around other people, and once again, more intrigued than ever, John wondered about her past. Was there a way to get over the wall she'd erected around herself? Why was it there in the first place? What was she hiding from?

He didn't have much time to think about his questions. In fifteen minutes they pulled up outside The Pines. The trip should have taken longer, he thought, as he put his pickup in park and turned off the engine. There was a world of difference between the complex where they lived and April Benoit's apartment.

Twenty units, maybe less, extended in a flat, one-story configuration. The roof gleamed and shimmered in the evening sun. It appeared new and had obviously just been replaced, but that only made the rest of the complex look worse. On the walls of the building, where the graffiti wasn't fresh, the paint was peeling and cracked. Lining the dilapidated sidewalk was a row of sad-looking plants, their last drink of water clearly weeks ago. The residents' cars, angled up to the doorways, looked as worn out as the rest of the place.

John climbed out of the pickup and walked up the sidewalk to where Elizabeth was waiting by the unit on the end. She seemed completely out of place, her long legs elegant, her black hair still in its sophisticated bun at the back of her neck. From a leather handbag, she pulled out a Mickey Mouse key ring. "It's not fancy," she warned.

"I think I can handle it," he said.

She unlocked the door and pushed it open. A musty odor assailed them, the sort of stale air that always made John's stomach flip. It never signified anything good. Reaching inside, Elizabeth turned on a light switch, but nothing happened.

She shook her head, clicking the lever back and

forth. "I guess the bill was due last week. I'll have to see about that."

She said the words without rancor, obviously accustomed to taking care of her sister.

John moved into the dim apartment behind her and looked around. It *was* messy, but a personality existed in the clutter. There was a minimum of furniture, but what was there looked clean and cared for. Colorful scatter rugs had been placed in strategic spots—to cover up worn linoleum, he was sure—and someone had taken the time to paint the walls a bright cheerful shade of pink. The color was echoed in several posters that hung over the sofa and a single overstuffed chair. Even in the poor light, he could see someone had tried.

"It's not that bad." He walked to the hallway and paused. "I've definitely seen worse."

Elizabeth stared at him through the gloom. "But she could do so much better. She makes good money and if she didn't waste half her salary on her friends, she could swing a better place. And if she couldn't—"

"You would help, right?"

"Yes," she answered defensively, "I would. What's wrong with that?"

"Nothing," he said, the dusky air between them filling with sudden tension, "if that's what your sister wanted."

She stood stock-still. "What's that supposed to mean?"

"It's not supposed to mean anything. It means what it means. If your sister wants your help, that's fine. If she doesn't, then she'd resent the hell out of you offering it all the time."

Elizabeth's shoulders slumped and she deflated like a balloon with a pin in its side. She sat down on the arm of the chair.

"She didn't want my help," she said woodenly. "That's exactly what we fought about the night of our birthday." She shook her head. "I didn't know, though. I thought I was doing the right thing. I knew she was independent and everything, but she came to me for help so often that I didn't think it was any different if I offered it myself." She looked up, a catch in her voice. "How was I supposed to know?"

He wanted to cross the tiny space between them and pull her into his arms, but he didn't. He simply stood in the doorway without moving, filled with sympathy. She loved her sister so much he could almost see the emotion. "She'd never told you before? Never gave you any clues?"

"No—at least, I don't think so. If she did, I certainly didn't catch them."

"Maybe she didn't want to hurt your feelings. Maybe she didn't know how to say it."

"Then why now?"

"I guess something must have changed."

For one long moment they looked at each other in the murky light, then he turned and went down the hall. In the bathroom he opened drawers, peered into the medicine chest, lifted the toilet lid. Nothing. Only more of the same in the bedroom. A sticky-sweet perfume lingered in the closet, hovering over the clothes. It was cloying, not at all like the light fresh scent Elizabeth wore. The clothes were totally different from hers, as well. Trendy bright colors and cheap fabric—certainly nothing that looked as if it came from Neiman's. He opened the drawer of the nightstand and reached inside. A conglomeration of junk took up most of the space—hand lotion, an old paperback mystery, a box of tissues. He pushed past the clutter and took out a small pink plastic container, lifting it by the edge. He popped it open carefully and studied the contents, then slipped it into his pocket.

He came back into the living room, walked past Elizabeth and went into the kitchen. The same routine there and the same results, too. Cans and microwave dinners. When he opened the refrigerator, a fetid odor rushed out full force. He read the date on the carton, then closed the door and went back into the living room.

"The last time you saw her was Sunday a week ago?"

She nodded.

"I don't think she came home after that. Milk's been bad almost three weeks." He reached into his pocket and took out the pink plastic container. "And I found these. Don't imagine she'd leave town without them, would she?"

Elizabeth recognized the package of birth control pills; they were the same brand she used. She cleared her throat and blinked, but her emotions won, and her eyes filled up. Fresh sympathy stabbed his heart, and John knelt in front of her, rocking back on his heels and steadying himself by putting his arm on her knees.

"I'm sorry," he said quietly. "I know this isn't easy for you. Can I get you a drink of water? Make you some coffee maybe?"

She sniffed. "I...I can get it."

Of course, she'd do it herself. Independent even in the throes of misery. He nodded, then moved back as she stood up and walked into the kitchen. Rising himself, he looked around the tiny living room. Just when he was thinking there was nothing much left to see, his eye caught a gleam of silver on a small end table. Crossing the space in a single stride, he picked up the expensive miniature frame and studied the photo inside.

Elizabeth's footsteps interrupted him, and without further thought, he dropped the frame and photo into his pocket. He turned and smiled at her. She held a can of soda. "It's warm, but there's another one. Would you like it?"

"I'll pass," he answered. "I think I've seen everything. Want to leave now?"

"I...I'd like to stay here for a little while. I want to straighten up a bit and clean out the refrigerator. There's no sense in leaving that mess to get even worse."

"It'll be too dark to see soon."

"I won't take long."

"Are you sure that's wise?" He waved a hand toward the parking lot. "This isn't your part of town."

"I know, but I'll be a half hour, tops." She smiled unexpectedly, and the effect was instantaneous. When John was only six, he'd picked up a live wire while his dad had been redoing a lamp. The same kind of electrical zing hit him right now. "You can check up on me. Watch my place. I'll turn on the lights when I get there. As a signal."

Through his reaction, he managed to realize the concession she was making. It was a crack—a very tiny crack—in the wall protecting her emotions. "You got a deal," he said. "I should be home—" he glanced down at his watch "—no later than nine. That'll be plenty of time to see Lisa and get back. How's that?"

She nodded. He was at the door and opening it when she called out his name.

He turned and looked across the pitiful room, struck once more by the incongruity of her appearance in this place. Her black hair was a shadow, her face a limned drawing of light and dark. She was so beautiful, so exotic, she almost didn't seem real.

"Yes?"

"Thanks." She paused. "Thanks for helping me."

He smiled and put his finger to the brim of his hat, then he turned around and left, his heart doing the sort of funny jig he hadn't felt in years.

ELIZABETH PULLED ASIDE the window curtain and watched John walk to his pickup and climb in. His movements were graceful and he walked with the smooth coordination of a man totally comfortable in his skin. He was probably a good dancer. She could imagine him in a Texas honky-tonk, doing the two-step, pushing that white hat back on his head, grinning that way he did. She turned abruptly and stared at the messy apartment. Cleaning out the refrigerator was all she needed to be thinking about. How great John Mallory looked when he moved was not important to her. Not important at all.

Heading with determination into the kitchen, Elizabeth opened the cabinet beneath the sink and removed a pair of rubber gloves. With a deliberately blank mind, she began to clean, starting with the countertops, wiping them down and tossing out a bag of moldy bread she found hiding behind the toaster. Scrubbing the sink took a little longer. The dishes stacked in the scratched and yellowed basin were crusted together with something she didn't want to think about. By the time she reached the refrigerator, it was almost too dark to see, but she didn't need her eyes. The smell alone was enough to guide her. Holding her breath, she took out everything she could get her hands on and tossed it into a plastic garbage bag she'd found in the pantry. She was closing the bag with a plastic tie when she heard something in the living room.

She stopped and listened. The noise repeated itself. A metal rattle, then a clicking. She couldn't immediately place the sounds, but when they registered a second later, her heart leapt. Someone was trying the doorknob.

April!

Before she could even run into the other room, Elizabeth realized her mistake. April would have a key. Besides that, she wouldn't be turning the knob so stealthily. John? Couldn't be. He'd knock or call out, just as anyone would do. No, this was someone else. Someone trying to get in who had no business here.

Her disappointment turned into alarm, then the alarm edged into panic. Had she been too busy staring at John, or had she locked the door? The soft clatter sounded a second time, and she held her breath, waiting for the squeaking hinges. When the noise didn't come, she realized, sick with relief, she must have thrown the dead bolt without even thinking. Whoever was on the other side was not getting in. At least not that way.

What to do?

It was almost completely dark now, inside the apartment and out. In the unit next door, the television set was at a stunning volume; they wouldn't hear her no matter how loudly she called out.

Trying to stay calm, Elizabeth forced herself to think. April had only one phone, and it was by the sofa in the living room. As softly as she could, Elizabeth set the plastic bag of refuse on the linoleum floor, then headed for the outer area, her footsteps as light as possible. At the doorway between the two rooms, she stopped suddenly, her pulse thumping, her mouth dry.

Someone was trying the door again. There was just enough light from the streetlamp outside filtering through the rippled glass window in the door to catch the gleaming metal as the knob twisted against its plate. A shadow moved, caught between the light and the window, and Elizabeth sucked in her breath. Whoever it was, he was big and tall with a dark wool cap pulled over his head. Ninety-five degrees outside, and he was wearing a ski mask.

Elizabeth didn't think twice. She reached behind her and felt blindly across the countertop, her eyes never leaving the door or its now-darkened window. Resting on the corner beside the refrigerator was the butcher-block knife holder she'd given April two years ago for Christmas. The shining Helger utensils were as sharp now as they'd been the day April had unwrapped them. Elizabeth's shaking fingers found the holder, and she pulled out a knife. Bringing it up close to her face, she stared at the razor sharp edge—she'd grabbed the meat carver.

Her stomach was in knots, but she crept forward through the darkness to the door. If she could get to the phone before whoever was on the other side of the door could get inside, she could dial 911.

Just as she had the thought, though, the knob jingled softly again, and she realized they weren't just trying the handle, they were jimmying the lock. She heard the soft sound of metal scraping metal as the pins were worked. With the knife in her hand and her heart in her throat, she reached for the receiver, stuck it between her jaw and shoulder, and dialed the numbers, her eyes still on the door.

The phone was dead.

They'd already cut the lines or the bill hadn't been paid, but either way it didn't matter. She'd get no help that way. Elizabeth swallowed a curse, then jerked her gaze back to the door. They'd given up on the lock and were going for the window, tapping it, testing its strength. A quiet second passed, then she heard a rasping sound. In horror she watched as the outside of the tiny paned window was covered with some kind of tape.

Her stomach gave a sickening lurch. They were going to punch out the window. When it broke, the tape would hold the shards in place. There would be no sound to alert anyone. Paralyzed with fear, Elizabeth stood and watched. A second later, a leather-gloved fist shot through the glass. The fingers fumbled for the lock and clicked it open.

The sound shattered her numbness. She lunged forward, knife raised. With one swift motion, she brought it down, the shining blade slicing through the leather as if it didn't exist.

A blood-chilling scream split the air.

CHAPTER FIVE

JOHN WATCHED his five-year-old daughter press her face against the yogurt counter, her expression one of complete indecision. Half afraid Marsha would change her mind and refuse him, he'd picked Lisa up and swept her off after leaving April's apartment. He'd made such a stink about the week before, Marsha had relented and allowed him to have Lisa an extra evening this week, but he had to take her home when they finished their outing. He wasn't too sure why Marsha had permitted him this additional time with his daughter. Was she mellowing after all this time? He doubted it, but anything was possible.

"Which flavor do you want, sweetheart?" he asked patiently. "Chocolate or vanilla?"

She shook her head, unable to pick while the line of customers behind them shifted restlessly. John smiled at the woman poised by the machine. "Give us one of each," he said, pulling out his wallet. "We might be here all night otherwise."

She grinned and pulled the levers, filling two white plastic dishes with the frozen dessert. John paid, then maneuvered Lisa to one of the tables near the window. She climbed happily into the nearest chair and held out both hands.

"You want them *both?*" he asked, laughing. "I thought I'd at least get one or the other."

"You like the pink kind," she said. "I like chocolate and vanilla."

He sat down beside her and put the cups in front of her. "You're a smart cookie for a five-year-old. Did you pull that trick on purpose?"

He melted faster than the yogurt as she sobered and shook her head seriously. "No, Daddy. No trick, I promise."

"Of course not," he answered, handing her two spoons. "You wouldn't do that." *Unlike your mother,* he thought.

Lisa dug happily into the chocolate, then added vanilla to the mound. Holding her mouth open as far as she could, she crammed the loaded spoon inside, getting most of the frozen yogurt in on the first try.

John leaned back and watched. He could sit there all evening and be perfectly happy, he realized. Everything Lisa did fascinated him, and it'd been that way since the day she was born. Marsha said he spoiled her, and maybe he did. But so what? Sometimes kids deserved a little spoiling.

He shifted slightly in the hard plastic chair, and the small silver-framed photo in his pocket reminded him of its presence. He straightened his leg and reached inside, removing the miniature holder. There had been two photos in it, one hidden below the other. He'd glanced at the bottom one, then taken it out and locked it in the glove compartment of his car for examination later. The one he held now was of two little girls, just about Lisa's age. He stared down at them and wondered if someone had spoiled Elizabeth and April Benoit. He hoped so.

"What's zat?"

"A picture," he answered. "Wanna see?"

Lisa nodded and reached out with a hand coated in yogurt.

He pulled it back and smiled. "How 'bout Daddy holds it and you look?"

"Okay."

He held the photograph in front of her.

"Who is it?"

"It's a lady I know and her sister. When they were about your age."

"What's their names?"

"Elizabeth and April. They're twins. Do you know what twins are?"

She nodded. "There's twins at school. Latesha and Kenisha."

John nodded. He'd seen the two little girls in her kindergarten class.

Lisa pointed her plastic spoon once more at the photo and frowned. "But they're not twins."

"What do you mean?"

"They aren't dressed the same."

He leaned closer to the table, putting his elbows on the top. "Well, not all twins do that, but they're still twins."

"How come?"

"Well, they both came out of their mommy's tummy at the same time."

She considered this for just a second, then nodded seriously. "Can I have a twin?"

"It's a tad late for that now, sweetie." *In more ways than one...* Marsha hadn't wanted children, period. He was damned lucky he had Lisa.

Obviously satisfied with his answer, his daughter returned to her yogurt, and John looked down at the photo again. It'd been taken at the beach, and the children in the picture were dressed in swimsuits—different ones. One was building a sand castle, a serious expression on her young face, the other one was frolicking in the waves. The snapshot had frozen her jumping a frothy turn of water and looking over her shoulder with a gleeful smile.

They looked exactly alike, but it was clear to him which one was which.

His thoughts turned to the other photo, the one locked in his car. It was of two young women with their arms around each other, their perfect bodies covered only minimally. Each wore an elaborate mask, feathered and sequined and large enough to cover most of their face. He'd believed at first it was a publicity shot April probably had done for herself and a friend, but the more he thought about it, the less sense that explanation made. Why would she keep a picture like that hidden in a sentimental frame, sitting in her apartment? No, it was a photograph that meant something to her, just as the one he now held between his fingers did. And why hide it? He was certain her actions had some significance. Maybe when he figured it out, he might figure out where April Benoit was, as well.

He hoped so, for Elizabeth's sake.

He allowed himself a few precious moments more to watch his daughter play with her spoon and leftover yogurt, then he reluctantly stood up. "Time to go, sweetheart," he said. "I promised your mom I'd bring you back, but I get to see you tomorrow, too. How's that? An extra day, huh?"

Lisa nodded happily, then scooted out of the chair. Fifteen minutes later they were at the house and walking up the sidewalk, Lisa's sticky fingers wrapped in his hand. Marsha opened the door before he could knock. With the barest of hellos, she pulled the little girl inside and closed the door. So much for mellowing.

As he climbed back into the truck, his mobile phone chirped. Picking it up, he hit the Send button and answered. "Mallory."

"John, this is Elizabeth Benoit. I'm sorry to bother you, but I didn't know who else to call...."

Her voice broke and his gut tightened. He knew what had happened. They'd found April. He'd told those clowns downtown to call him if that happened—not Elizabeth—but they could never get anything right. "What is it?" he said, anyway. "What's wrong?"

"You'd better come back to April's place. There's..." He heard her take a sharp breath, then, "There's blood everywhere and I...I don't know what to do. I stabbed someone, John."

ON THE STREET outside April's apartment, Elizabeth was waiting in her car—*locked* in her car—when John pulled up, his brakes squealing as he slammed to a halt and parked right beside her. He jumped out while the truck was still rocking to a stop. She opened her own door and met him halfway. Her heart had slowed its wild pounding and had changed into a steady battering rate, but she was operating on pure adrenaline, nothing else. God, she was glad to see him! Too glad.

He put his hands on her shoulders. "First things first," he said calmly. "Are you all right? Are you hurt?"

She shook her head. "I'm fine."

"So that blood isn't yours?"

She looked down at her T-shirt and cringed. "N-no. It's not mine."

"Who does it belong to?"

"I...I have no idea. I was cleaning up when someone broke into the apartment. I grabbed a kitchen knife and stabbed him. Then he ran off."

"Have you called 911?"

"Yes. I phoned them from the manager's office just before I called you. I guess I could have let them handle it, but I thought—"

"You did the right thing, Elizabeth. Exactly the right thing." The look in his brown eyes warmed her. "I'm glad you called me."

She nodded, but before she could say more, a blue-and-white cruiser pulled up. Two uniformed patrolmen, holding clipboards, got out of the car and came toward them as John pulled his badge from his pocket to show them.

Elizabeth started to explain, but one of the men stopped her. "Let's go inside," he said, tilting his head to the bystanders who'd already gathered. "I don't think we need an audience, do we?"

They entered April's apartment, Elizabeth stepping gingerly over the spots of blood near the door as the officers shone their flashlights on it. The knife lay on the floor where she'd dropped it, and the broken glass told the rest of the story. She elaborated on what had happened to the three men.

"He fled after you stabbed him?"

"Y-yes. He screamed, pulled his hand back through the window and ran. I followed him outside, but it was too dark to see anything. He…he was big, though, and tall. Dressed completely in black with a ski mask."

"You followed him out the door?" The officer looked at her in amazement.

"Well, yes. Wh-what else was I supposed to do?"

He raised his eyebrows, looked at his partner and shrugged. Muttering that it was a "good thing she didn't have a gun," the two men began to examine the doorframe and the area outside, their radios softly chattering.

John moved closer to where she stood in the doorway. "Are you positive you didn't know who this was? Think hard."

She shook her head. "It must have just been a burglar. I'm sure the neighbors realized April hasn't been here. Maybe it was too good an opportunity to pass up."

His face turned thoughtful. "Has her place been broken into before?"

"Yes. More than once actually. That's why she doesn't even keep a TV anymore."

Elizabeth looked up as one of the uniformed officers approached.

He pushed his hat back on his head. "Ma'am,

we'll make a report on this, but we're not too hopeful of finding the guy.''

She sent John a look, but all he did was shrug.

''I can call for a crime scene unit to come over,'' the cop continued. ''They'll get the blood type and look for prints, call the hospitals and check for stab-wound victims—but you'll have to wait here for them. They'll need someone to secure the place after they leave, and since it's Friday night, they probably won't get here for hours.''

Her indecision must have shown; John spoke up. ''Why don't you turn in the report and we'll lock up the place the best we can for now? In the morning, if we decide to pursue it, I'll call in the CSU guys and handle it myself. How's that?''

The uniformed man looked uncertain. John's suggestion wasn't standard operating procedure.

''Morris!'' From behind them, the other cop spoke suddenly, his finger on the mike by his collar. ''Gotta call down on Westheimer. We need to roll. Now, man. C'mon!''

There was no longer a choice. The cop beside them started running backward. ''I'll call you with the case number, Detective.'' He dipped his head in Elizabeth's direction. ''Sorry for your troubles, ma'am. Take care.''

They disappeared a second later, their red and blue lights cutting into the darkness as they sped away.

JOHN INSISTED on driving Elizabeth home himself, and by the time they got back to their condo complex, Elizabeth was glad. Somewhere on the freeway she'd begun to shiver and couldn't seem to stop.

He took one look at her, put his arm around her and led her to her unit. When they reached the door, he took her key from her trembling fingers and opened it himself, stepping aside as they entered.

"Go take a bath," he said. "As hot as you can stand it. I'm going to fix us something to eat and get you a drink, too."

She looked up at him. "You don't have to do this, John."

Ignoring her protest, he put his hands on her shoulders and turned her in the direction of the hallway. "Go get out of those clothes. Take a bath. It'll help."

Elizabeth was not accustomed to anyone telling her what to do, but she didn't have the strength to argue. She wasn't used to stabbing people, either. She walked down the hall with one hand against the wall and entered the bathroom, closing the door behind her.

Twenty minutes later she heard a tap on the bathroom door. "You okay in there?"

Sitting in the tub, steam floating around her, Elizabeth realized she'd finally stopped shaking, and, in fact, had almost begun to doze—a reaction, she was sure, to the sudden drain of energy. She opened her eyes and answered, "Yes. I'm almost finished."

The door opened about four inches, and John's hand snaked through with a tumbler half-full of amber liquid and set it on the countertop. "Drink this," he said through the door, which he'd quickly reclosed. "Dinner's almost ready."

She got out of the tub, toweled dry and reached for the glass. The Scotch tasted ambrosial, and by the time she'd brushed her hair and stuck her arms into her full-length terry cloth robe, she felt almost human again. With her hand on the doorknob, she paused and looked back at her reflection in the mirror. She had an incredibly gorgeous man in her kitchen cooking her dinner and she was going to walk in there looking like this?

It doesn't matter, a stern voice inside her answered. *He's only helping you out, nothing more. You don't want anything more, remember?*

She picked up the glass, drained the Scotch, then opened the door. The first thing she noticed was the smell of something wonderful. It pulled her down the hall and into the kitchen where she stopped abruptly in the doorway. John was standing in front of the stove, stirring, his back to her.

"Come in," he said, without turning. "Dinner's almost ready."

She shook her head. "You read minds *and* have

eyes in the back of your head? Your little girl's going to hate that when she's a teenager.''

He turned around and grinned, wiping his hands on a kitchen towel he'd tucked into the waistband of his jeans. ''She hates it now,'' he answered. ''But maybe she'll be used to it by the time she turns sixteen.''

They smiled at each other across the room, then his gaze made a sweeping perusal of her, from tousled hair to terry robe to toes peeking out from beneath the hem. When he met her eyes again, the rubbery sensation in her legs was threatening to return, but this time for a whole different reason.

''You look better,'' he said quietly. ''I thought I was gonna lose you back there at April's.''

''I felt pretty shaky.''

''You *looked* pretty shaky.'' His gaze drifted over her again, then finally came to rest on her face. ''But Scotch has remarkably restorative qualities. Would you like another?''

''No, thank you.'' She put the glass on the counter. ''One's my limit.''

He nodded, then turned back to the stove. ''All right, then go sit down and I'll bring you my one and only specialty.''

Elizabeth did as he asked, and a moment later he came to the table with two steaming plates. When he set one in front of her, her mouth started to water. A Denver omelet, just the way she preferred it, with crisp bacon on the side and two slices of toast—cut on the diagonal.

"This looks fantastic. You made this out of the stuff in my refrigerator?"

He sat down beside her and nodded. "I found a green pepper and some onions hiding in the back. You don't cook, do you?"

Picking up her fork, she shook her head. "Not really. I do salads, sandwiches, stuff like that. I eat out mostly." She took a bite of the omelet and closed her eyes. "Mmm."

"I'm glad you approve." He tucked into his own. "As I said, this is my only specialty. I don't like to spread my talent too thin."

Elizabeth chuckled and they ate in companionable silence. By the time their plates were clean, Elizabeth felt almost herself again.

Then she remembered the blood.

She put down her knife and fork and reached for the coffee mug, wrapping her suddenly cold fingers around it.

"This thing…at April's…" she asked shakily, "do you think it was a random break-in or someone she knew?"

"I don't know. Either way's a possibility." He pushed away his own plate and looked at her. "But if she didn't just walk away, the break-in could very well be connected to her disappearance."

Elizabeth's throat tightened. She couldn't believe

they were talking this way about April. About her twin. The whole thing had such a nightmarish quality. "And if she didn't just leave…"

He hesitated.

"I can take it," she said. "Just tell me. I need to know what we're really dealing with if she didn't go away on her own."

He nodded reluctantly. "Well, worst case, a nut could have grabbed her for some reason—her purse, her looks, because she reminded him of his mother, who knows—and now she's dead. He could have taken your car, along with her, and either sold it or chopped it. I've been checking on it, but no sign yet."

Elizabeth took a sip of coffee. It tasted bitter, but not because it wasn't well-made. She forced herself to swallow. "Go on."

"Next possibility—someone grabbed her, but she's still alive. Again a nut case with a weird motive. But then, I'd expect the car to turn up."

He raised his hand and held up his fingers to indicate a third and fourth option. "Or, someone who *knows* her did either of the above. Kidnapped her or killed her for a reason only the two of them understand."

"What's your best guess?"

His voice went flat and hard. "Eighty percent of all homicides are committed by people who know their victims. That leaves twenty percent done by strangers. More women are sent to the emergency room by their husbands or boyfriends than from car accidents, robberies and rapes combined.''

''My God!'' Elizabeth's voice was a horrified whisper. ''How can that be?''

His expression shifted again, and something dark and ominous replaced his usual calm countenance. ''It's all about control,'' he answered. ''We like power. But when the need for it gets too extreme, bad things happen.'' He stared down into his mug for a moment, then he raised his face and asked. ''Who would want to control your sister, Elizabeth? Who had the power over her?''

She answered instantly. ''Greg Lansing. He was her boss and her boyfriend. A double whammy.''

''I thought they weren't dating anymore.''

''That's what *he* said, but I don't know that for a fact. She wasn't dating anyone else—or she would have told me.''

''Did she ever say anything about going out with men she met at the club?''

''She didn't date customers. We both knew it was dangerous. I…I made her promise she'd never do that. Why do you ask?''

''Seems to be a lot of money floating around there. If I were her and one of those customers with a Rolls asked me out, I might be tempted.''

''Not April. She makes a lot and she spends a lot. Money means nothing to her.''

"Are you sure?"

Something in his voice made her stop and think. *Was* she sure? April had changed since they'd come to Houston. The guy she'd gone to the Caribbean with—he'd been a customer, hadn't he? Maybe John was right. He'd asked her once before how close she and April really were. Maybe she didn't really know her sister as well as she thought she did. Or as well as she had in the past. At a certain point their lives had separated and they'd each taken a different direction.

"I don't know," Elizabeth answered quietly.

"I tried calling Tracy Kensington yesterday to set up that appointment, but never got an answer. I'm not sure if she knows anything or not, but I'd like to talk to her again."

"She might know something," Elizabeth was now willing to concede, "but she'd never tell you. The dancers don't feel comfortable around people outside the business. They have a closed community—like cops. They're in a different world from everyone else. Working at night, sleeping all day. Most of them don't even tell anyone what they do." She shrugged. "It can be a very lonely life. Very isolating. It's…not a good place to be. At least, I don't think so." She shook her head. "You'll never get Tracy to tell you if April was going out with a customer—or anything else for that matter."

"Despite what she said?"

Nodding, Elizabeth spoke without thinking. "She saw you in the club, took a good look and decided she wanted a piece of it, that's all." Immediately she snapped her mouth shut and cursed herself silently. The thought—and the way she'd expressed it—was not how an attorney would think and talk, was it? Without even being aware of it, she was slipping back, back to a place and a time she wanted to forget.

If John noticed, he didn't let on. His expression didn't change, not one iota, but that didn't mean a thing. John Mallory was sharper than any man she'd ever met. If he could read her mind as he seemed able to do, it wasn't a great leap for him to see her past. She got up abruptly and walked into the kitchen, carrying her cup and plate to the dishwasher. Standing at the sink, she closed her eyes.

All at once his voice sounded right in her ear, and her eyes flew open. Just as he had that time at the gym, he'd moved clear across the room without making a sound, and now he was standing so close she could see a scar halfway down his right temple, a tiny crescent moon. Her eyes met his.

"You've told me all you know, haven't you, Elizabeth? You aren't holding anything back on me, are you?"

"L-like what?"

"I don't know." He reached out unexpectedly and brushed a stray lock of hair from her face. It was a perfectly innocent gesture. He made no other move to touch her. "I don't know," he repeated, "but sometimes when I look at you, I think you have secrets. What are you hiding?"

"Nothing. Why would I want to?"

His voice was a low rumble. "Why don't you tell me?"

She forced herself to laugh lightly. "I think you've been interrogating too many suspects, Detective. There *are* people in the world without secrets, you know."

"I've been told that," he said evenly, "but I've yet to meet one."

He left a few minutes later. She closed and locked the door behind him and then watched as he crossed the space between his town house and hers with the same easy grace she'd seen before. This time, though, she stared at him with a shiver of fear alongside her interest. What kind of beast had she let out of its cage?

JOHN MADE UP HIS MIND the minute he left Elizabeth's apartment. He stopped by his place first and arranged to have someone retrieve her car, then he told the dispatcher where he was going. Fifteen minutes later he was heading down the Richmond strip.

Even though it was a weeknight, the club's parking lot was as packed as ever, but John paid little attention this time. Once inside, he found the hostess and gave her his best big-spender grin. She was a brunette tonight, but just as beautiful as the blonde had been last Friday. "Find Tracy Kensington for me, would you, doll?" he said, pressing some bills into her hand. "I need her real bad."

"Sure thing, cowboy." She tucked the money into the vee of her blouse and grinned. "That's easy money. She's dancing in the second room. On your left."

He headed down the hallway to the bar with the black walls and mirrors, but just as he entered, the room went totally dark. He stood where he was, by the doorway, until the lights came up again suddenly, a spot on each table and a single stronger one on the stage. The effect was dramatic. John didn't know where to look first.

There was a woman on every table, and front and center was Tracy Kensington.

The music began; Tina Turner making promises. John made his way through the haze of smoke and maze of tables to stand near the stage.

She saw him immediately. Grabbing the pole nearest the edge of the stage, she wound herself around it, her red hair flying, her eyes sparking with an emotion he couldn't read.

"We need to talk," he said.

"Not here." She spoke above the music, just to him. "I told you to call me at home."

"I tried. You didn't answer."

She lifted one long leg and tucked it close to the pole, her eyes darting nervously over the room. Her mood wasn't as open or playful as it had been the last time. In fact, he thought, she looked downright scared. But she smiled at him invitingly and batted her eyes in fake interest. "I don't want to talk to you here."

He reached into his pocket and pulled out some bills to keep up the pretense himself. "Why not?"

"I just don't. I can't." Using her arms as levers, she lifted herself easily and swung to the other side of the pole. It was a practiced move and smoothly executed. Her titian hair brushed his face. When she landed, she said, "Leave. Please…just leave."

He ignored the plea and tucked a twenty into the silken strap of her G-string. "Tell me what you know about April."

"Didn't you hear what I said?"

"I heard you, Tracy, but I don't want to do it that way. So you can talk to me here, or we can go down to Travis Street."

Her eyes widened, and for the first time, she faltered. She caught herself instantly, the staggeringly high heels clicking against the stage. "The station? No way, man."

He leaned closer. "I know all about the private dances you do in the back, Tracy." Raising one eyebrow, he left the unspoken threat hanging in the smoky air between them.

"You aren't being fair—"

"Life isn't. So finish your set, then talk to me. It won't take five minutes, I promise."

Swinging away from him, she moved to the other side of the stage and continued her show, the men crowding around, all anxious to give her money. From above their heads, her eyes pierced John's. This time he could read her gaze easily. She was scared. Scared to death.

The music stopped a few minutes later, and the women all disappeared, Tracy with them. John cursed loudly, then he saw her. She was getting a robe from someone standing offstage. She slipped into the short terry garment, then came over to his table and sat. The bar girl immediately appeared, but John handed her a wad of bills and waved her off.

He spoke without preliminaries. "What do you know about April's disappearance? For real. Not just conjecture."

"I don't know anything," she said.

"You seemed mighty sure you knew something the other night when I was here. Was it about April going out with customers?"

"She didn't go out with customers."

"That's what Elizabeth said. But Greg seemed to think she might. In fact, he told me she did."

Tracy shot a quick glance toward the bar. "He would."

John leaned closer, crossing his arms and putting his elbows on the table. "Why would Greg Lansing want to do that? Did he have something to do with April's disappearance?"

"No!" She began to chew on her thumbnail, then seemed to realize what she was doing and dropped her hand back into her lap. "Talking to you was dumb, okay? I shouldn't have said anything in the first place."

"But you had something you wanted to say, didn't you?"

She stayed silent.

He leaned closer. "I'll find out, Tracy, one way or the other. Make it easy on yourself and tell me now."

"I don't have to tell you anything."

"No, but you'll wish you had if we have to go downtown."

He noticed beads of perspiration dotting her full upper lip. "Look," she said, "I was just trying to get a rise out of you, that's all."

"I don't believe you," he said bluntly. "I think you had something you wanted to tell me and now, for some reason, you've changed your mind."

She was shaking her head before he finished, the red hair tumbling over her shoulders in a tangle.

"You're wrong. I don't know anything about it, okay? Nothing."

"April didn't talk to you? Didn't say anything about going somewhere? Who was she dating, Tracy? Did you ever see her with someone? Maybe someone from around here?"

"I don't know!"

"What about Lansing? Was he still going out with April?"

She couldn't have jumped up faster if he'd hit her with a cattle prod. "This is stupid. I said I don't know anything, and I mean it." Her gaze bounced nervously around the bar before landing on him again. "Don't come back here and ask me questions like this, either. It's not helping you, and it's definitely not helping me." She turned and almost ran from the room.

John's eyes followed her, and he couldn't help but remember Elizabeth's words. Had Tracy been scamming him or had she changed her mind? Had someone else changed her mind for her? Standing up, John went back to the club entrance and found the brunette. "Greg working tonight?" he asked casually.

"Sure is. Just saw him. You want me to get him for you, too?" She arched one perfect brow and grinned.

He shook his head. "That's okay, honey. Just checking."

"Anytime," she purred. "Anytime, cowboy."

CHAPTER SIX

"YOU'VE TOLD me all you know, haven't you, Elizabeth?"

John's words rang in Elizabeth's mind as she got dressed for work the following morning. As she stood in front of the bathroom mirror fixing the bun at the nape of her neck, she also remembered his expression. The warm brown eyes had reflected skepticism, and the lie she'd given him as an answer had left a bad taste in her mouth, which was still there.

She closed her eyes for a second, but when she opened them again, the same face was staring back at her from the mirror. The same deceptive face.

Turning away, Elizabeth stalked into her bedroom, grabbed her briefcase from the desk by her bed and walked quickly into her living room. How had life gotten so complicated so fast? Two weeks ago, everything had been perfectly all right, and now it was going to hell.

Thanks, April.

Climbing into her rental car, Elizabeth immediately felt guilty. Something terrible might have happened to her sister, and here she was, angry at her. April was the only family Elizabeth had! She berated herself a moment longer, but then let up and acknowledged that it was only human to harbor some resentment. It seemed as if she'd spent most of her life taking care of April's problems—and their mother's. It'd sure be nice for a change if someone took care of *her* problems.

Someone was, or was trying to, a little voice inside said. John Mallory.

Getting on the freeway and pointing the car downtown, Elizabeth thought about the night before. John had been incredibly kind and supportive, but for the first time she'd seen something in those dark eyes that told her he might have some secrets, too. What *was* behind his motivation to help her? When he'd recited his murder statistics, a coldness had come over him he hadn't been able to hide. She couldn't help but wonder if someone he knew had been hurt, someone in his family. She shivered slightly and reached over to switch off the air-conditioning that suddenly seemed unnecessary.

Whatever his motivation, he certainly was trying, she had to admit, and when she'd seen his long lean form stride up to her at April's apartment last night, she'd felt a reaction she couldn't deny. He had a calm, soothing air about him that made her want to know him better in spite of herself.

But she couldn't.

She couldn't because she didn't want to, and she couldn't because...well, she just couldn't. He'd uncover her secrets, and once he knew them, John Mallory would never be able to get past them. And he *would* learn them, she was sure. Sooner or later he'd know. Everything.

Elizabeth didn't want to fool herself. She was still on her own, and it'd be a mistake to think otherwise. She could depend on no one but herself to find out what had happened to April.

Elizabeth turned the problem over in her mind one more time. John had done the logical thing by going to April's apartment, even though April didn't keep anything important there. As the burglary attempt had proved, the place wasn't safe, and her twin had known it. Elizabeth had called the police, but no progress had been made on finding out who'd attempted to break in. It was a high-crime area— the police didn't have time to investigate every little burglary. April had known this, too. She'd told Elizabeth once that whenever she had something to hide, she took it to the club.

It was a moment before that thought registered, but when it did, Elizabeth smacked the steering wheel with the palm of her hand. Of course! She should have gone to the Esquire first thing and looked in April's locker. She knew the combination; they always used the same code for everything— their mother's birthday. If she'd planned a trip, there might be some hint of it there, notes about airline schedules or something along those lines.

Ignoring the honking horns behind her, Elizabeth jerked the car into the right lane and exited the freeway a moment later. Winding her way through the backstreets, she pulled into the almost empty parking lot of the club ten minutes later. A single white BMW sat forlornly near the now-darkened neon sign, obviously abandoned, its owner someone who'd apparently thought better of driving himself home the night before. Staring at the car, she realized at once what a waste of time her hasty trip was. What had she been thinking? There would be no one at the club this early in the morning. They'd probably left only a few hours before.

She stared dejectedly at the elaborate facade of the building. It looked garish and false in the morning's bright sunlight. She'd only been in there once. She'd wanted to see April dance, and without telling her, she'd slipped inside late one night, wearing dark glasses and a cheap dress she'd thrown away later. She didn't have a good reason for all the secrecy, but she hadn't wanted April to know she was there. The explanation would have just been too…complicated.

She started the car and got back on the freeway. It was noon before she had the chance to call the club.

"Esquire Club."

"Tracy, this is Elizabeth Benoit. I was wondering if—"

The dancer interrupted brusquely. "Look, I told that detective last night I don't know anything about your sister, okay? I can't tell you what I don't know."

It took a second for Elizabeth to realize what had happened. John must have called or shown up, and Tracy had brushed him off, just as Elizabeth had predicted. So instead of asking about April's locker as she'd planned, Elizabeth decided to play along. "That's what John told me, Tracy, but I know differently. April said she talked to you."

"She did?" The dancer's voice rose in disbelief. "Well…she was lying. I didn't talk to her about anything. She was lying," she repeated.

"I think *you're* the one who's lying."

"I don't give a damn *what* you think. I don't know anything about April and I have no idea where she is. You can sit up there all high and mighty in your pristine little office, but I don't have anything to say to you, *Miz* Benoit."

Elizabeth could imagine Tracy's expression. She was happy April was gone and happy Elizabeth was upset about it.

"Tracy, look…I'm not trying to give you a hard time, I just want to know where my sister is. I'm worried sick about her. Are you sure you don't know anything?"

The dancer's voice changed again, the words now clipped and cold. "I *told* him I don't know anything, and I'm telling you the same."

"What about the other girls?"

"I don't know."

"Would you ask them for me?"

"You want to know, you ask them."

"Right." Elizabeth squeezed the bridge of her nose, feeling a rush of disappointment. "I'm sure that'd be really helpful. They'll tell me just as much as you have."

There was a short tense silence, then Tracy spoke again. "If you think I'm going to help you, you're crazier than that cop you sent down here. I've got three little words for you, Miss Benoit, and they are Go. To. Hell."

The next thing Elizabeth heard was a click. Tracy had hung up.

Tracy would never tell her anything.

The other girls would never tell her anything.

And Greg Lansing sure as hell wouldn't tell her anything.

They had their own little world and nothing was going to penetrate it. John couldn't without a warrant, and Elizabeth couldn't, period. They were outsiders. Not welcome.

Elizabeth stared out the window. She was accustomed to dealing with numbers, columns, things that either added up or didn't. Mentally she stepped back from the situation and looked at it through different eyes.

And the answer came almost instantly.

And she rejected it just as fast.

No way. Forget it. Uh-uh.

Elizabeth concentrated, instead, on her work, calling Linda Tremont to get a few more details she needed for her report. Talking to the older woman, Elizabeth answered her sympathetic questions about April. Then she hung up and began to study a new case.

But late that night, when she couldn't get to sleep, Elizabeth's mind returned to April. She had to find her. Nothing else was important. April couldn't take care of herself as Elizabeth could, and just like their mother, April needed Elizabeth, whether she knew it or not.

The hot sting of tears gathered in her suddenly tight throat. Dammit to hell, she needed April, too. What would she be if she wasn't April's sister? They couldn't read each other's minds anymore, but in a complex and unexplainable way, they still defined each other, always had, always would.

Elizabeth sat up in bed and glanced at the clock—2:00 a.m.—then stared at the wall. There was a crape myrtle tree just outside the window, and a breeze made the branches tangle with each other in a shadowy dance and scratch against the glass. It was a troubling sound and one that took her into the past.

Just after her father died, Elizabeth had had an absolutely horrible nightmare. Even with sixteen years between the reality and the memory, she shivered as she remembered. She'd dreamed she was in an earthquake, the ground beneath her shifting and collapsing, everything around her, familiar and loved, disappearing into a dark abyss. The sensation of sliding away had been so terrifying she could still remember her heart slamming against her chest. She'd never had a dream—before or since—that had left her feeling so out of control.

Screaming and thrashing, she'd woken up to April's voice, her sister's arms around her, her hands patting her lovingly on the back. "It's okay, Elizabeth. It's okay. I'm here." Elizabeth's relief had been so great, she'd immediately broken into a flood of tears. April had held her until she'd gone back to sleep, and the next morning, April had just smiled at her. They'd never mentioned what had happened. Why she thought of it now, she had no idea, but the recollection swept over her in a rush of memory so sweet and real it took her breath away.

She needed April and April needed her.

Before she could think about it more, in the dim darkness of her bedroom, Elizabeth reached for her phone and punched out a number.

JOHN REPLACED the receiver and tried to remain calm. Just because he'd been calling Elizabeth all evening long and she hadn't answered was no good reason to panic. It was Saturday night after all. She was a beautiful woman who must have more than her share of dates. Her sister's disappearance didn't mean Elizabeth had to put her entire life on hold. She'd probably gone out to dinner or a movie, or just out for drinks. She didn't have to report to him.

Sitting at his desk in the crowded squad room, he snorted at his logic. Who was he kidding? He knew how much April meant to Elizabeth. If she wasn't at home, she was out trying to find her sister. He hoped she hadn't gone back to the apartment. He'd tried to stay cool about the break-in, but something told him it hadn't been a random thing.

He thought of Tracy Kensington's worried expression. Why did he get the feeling the answers he needed were at the Esquire Club?

Because something weird was going on there, he told himself. Something really weird.

The grand chandelier, the polished wood floors, the aura of wealth and privilege didn't fool him a bit. The Esquire Club was just another strip joint, and underneath its glittering facade was the same dirt you'd find in any such place. Drugs. Gambling. Private dances that led to something else. The patrons might drive expensive cars and smoke cigars that would cost John a week's salary, but they were really no different from the people in other places, where the drinks were cheap and the dancers older. People on the edge. People who weren't quite on the up and up. People who craved the thrill and the rush. April's disappearance had to be tied to that club. It had to be.

He glanced at his watch, then threw down the pencil he'd been gnawing on and jumped to his feet. Grabbing his hat, he strode from the office.

ELIZABETH HAD CALLED and ordered the electricity restored to April's apartment the day after the break-in. She'd also had the window repaired. Standing on the sidewalk Saturday evening, she unlocked the new dead bolt she'd also had installed, then reached around the open door and flipped on the lights. When the overhead fixture sputtered on and flooded the living room with dim illumination, she stepped inside.

She didn't have much time. She'd put off coming until the very last minute, and as her gaze went to the floor, she knew why. The manager had sent the super over to scrub the cracked linoleum, but it hadn't done much good. Elizabeth could still see the blood splatters. She swallowed, her mouth suddenly dry. Had it been a random crime or something more sinister? She didn't want to think about it.

Moving quickly past the stain, Elizabeth went directly to April's bedroom and opened the door to the closet. She paused for a moment in front of the bi-level poles, then she lifted a trembling hand and pushed the crowded hangers back and forth. It only took a minute for her to find what she was looking for. Just as she'd suspected, April had kept the mask.

Elizabeth's fingers shook even more as she reached out for the feathered headdress, and when she brushed the silky plumage, it was all she could do to not cry out and pull back. The simple sensation of the feathers against her hand had ignited a memory that seared her with its intensity. Everything rushed in at once. The pounding music. The haze of smoke. The leering faces. The crude calls. She pulled the mask from its hanger and stepped out of the suddenly claustrophobic confines of the closet.

The bedroom was tiny, but the two steps she took to get to the mirror on the other side of the room were enormous. When she got there and stood in front of the glass, the woman looking back at her wasn't the same woman who'd walked into the room a few seconds before.

She was a terrified seventeen-year-old. Hungry, completely broke, nothing left of what she'd been before except her pride—and that was disappearing almost before her eyes.

A moan escaped her lips and Elizabeth sank down to the bed behind her, her legs giving out, the de-

termined resolution that had brought her here fleeing
as well.

What in the hell did she think she was doing?

She clutched the mask and rocked back and forth.
"I can't do this." The words sounded heavy in the
lifeless air. "I really can't do this. Not again."

She'd come so far, done so much...and now it
was back to this? Elizabeth shook her head, the
feathers hot, the sequins heavy in her now sweaty
hands. It wouldn't work, anyway. She had to actually get hired, and then she had to get in with the
girls—and fast. And what if they really didn't know
anything after all? It was a hare-brained scheme, she
told herself. Something April would do—not her.

Elizabeth sat quietly on the edge of the bed for a
few more seconds, then she gathered her determination, took a big breath and stood up. Stepping to
the mirror, she lifted the mask and put it in front
her face, the thin elastic strap that held it on going
over her head, the clips on either side sinking into
her hair. She adjusted it slightly, then dropped her
hands to her side and stared at her reflection.

The mask was made of heavy white silk, shot
through with gold and silver threads. It served as a
base for the white plumes that arched above her
eyes and all the way down the side, curving grace-
fully to hide most of her face. Sequins in graduated
circles of blue ringed the eyes. At the outermost
part, they were light blue, but as they came closer

to her eyes, they got darker and darker. The inner circle of sparkles was the darkest shade of midnight—almost, but not quite, black. Behind the slanted openings, her gaze glittered bright and hot. It was hard to see where the sequins stopped and her eyes began.

She stared until the image in the mirror wavered, then she lifted off the mask and laid it gently on the bed. Going back to the closet, she shifted the hangers some more and found the rest of the outfit. It was pressed and clean and looked as ready for use as it had been a few years ago. Elizabeth shut down the part of her brain that was screaming in protest, and carefully lifted the glittering costume out of the closet, along with the headdress and high heels that went with it. Moments later she had it all zippered into the plastic garment bag she'd brought with her. Laying it back on the bed, she went into April's bathroom and opened the cabinet doors beneath the lavatory.

April's makeup was right where she always kept it. Elizabeth pulled out the black leather chest and opened the lid. Inside was a wide assortment of foundations, lipsticks, eye shadows and blushes. The colors were more dramatic than any Elizabeth wore now, and, washing her face, she carefully reapplied her makeup using her sister's cosmetics, working fast and efficiently. When she'd finished and stepped back, the effect was startling.

This time, the woman in the mirror was more than different; she was a complete and utter stranger. Gone was anyone who would be recognized, especially a conservatively dressed consultant who specialized in tax law. In her place was an exotic beauty, eyes heavy with mascara and smoky shadow, cheeks hollowed dramatically with a brownish blush. Lush red pouty lips finished the look.

Still staring at the stranger in the mirror, she said, "I'm here for the job." No, that wasn't right. Elizabeth tried again, more breathlessly this time. "I called earlier...." As if shaking loose the last of her former self, she closed her eyes and tossed her head slightly. Imagining the man she'd have to convince, she stayed perfectly still for one long moment, then opened her eyes and spoke once more, this time her voice a gravelly drawl, her gaze almost sizzling.

"I'm Lizzie Bennet." Two beats and a longer pause, the self-confidence too strong to ignore. "I believe you're short one dancer?"

JOHN ANGLED his pickup into a parallel spot on Richmond that a BMW was vacating. He got out quickly, locked the vehicle and strode toward the front door of the Esquire.

If he thought the club had been busy before, tonight it was jammed. The smell of smoke and expensive perfume was almost overpowering, and everyone looked as well-heeled as they had on his previous visits. But this time John saw through the facade immediately. He saw the desperation on the faces of some of the women and the avaricious gleam in the eyes of the men. Why did they come here? he wondered. What were they searching for?

He was halfway down the dark hall to Greg Lansing's office when he heard his name called out. Glancing left, then right, John spotted the rowdy group of detectives in the room that resembled a smoking den. He groaned. There was nothing to do but head their way. If he didn't, he'd never hear the end of it.

"Hey, Mallory, what the hell you doing here?" Pat Ricker, one of the homicide detectives, lifted his glass of beer as John reached the table full of men. "Didn't figure this was your kind of place!"

John smiled at him and the rest of the group. He recognized most and nodded to the ones he didn't, his gaze coming back to rest on Ricker's. It was easier to go along with the ribbing than it was to explain his presence. "Well, you figured wrong, buddy. I come here all the time. It's my favorite. I know all the girls!"

The men snickered, and one of the younger ones sitting near the stage spoke up. "Just how well do you know 'em, Mallory?" Not waiting for an answer, he continued after a conspiratorial glance at the others. "You used to be in Vice, right? All kinds of benefits there, I hear…"

John played along till he remembered the younger man's name. "That's right, Dixon, and when you start to shave, I'll tell you about 'em some day."

They laughed, then tried to get him to sit with them. John held up his hands. "I'd love to, guys, but I've got to see someone…"

They all began to talk at once. "Yeah, yeah. Sure you do!"

"The redhead or the blonde?"

"It's the brunette, I'll bet…"

John grinned and started to answer, but the lights in the room unexpectedly dimmed and a woman's voice spoke from the loudspeakers near the stage. "The Esquire Club is proud to present a new dancer this evening. Straight from New Orleans…Madame Leda! Give her a warm welcome, ladies and gentlemen."

The room went completely dark, and John was trapped. If he tried to leave now, he'd trip over the nearest table. Behind him someone yelled, "Sit down up there!" and all he could do was take the chair someone pushed behind his knee.

His eyes swung to the stage. A single spotlight was focusing on the floor and moving slowly upwards. Up and over a pair of white spike heels, up and over legs that seemed to go on forever…up and over a body so tantalizingly covered in a see-through gown that John suddenly lost all interest in leaving.

The room had fallen totally silent, the woman's face still hidden in darkness. Out of the quiet, the first beats of music began. It was an old Eagles song, ''Witchy Woman,'' slow and sensual with a count so steady and rhythmic John felt an answering cadence pulse inside him. Like everyone else in the room, he was totally mesmerized as the light continued its inexorable journey upward.

When the beam fully revealed the dancer, John let out the breath he'd been holding.

The upper half of her face was covered by a Mardi Gras style mask, complete with feathers and sequins. It revealed nothing about the woman but her eyes. Behind the two black holes, surrounded by the rings of glitter, she stared out at the crowd. Beneath a diaphanous white robe, she wore a glittering G-string and two white pasties, her full round breasts shadowed beneath the robe, all the more sensuous since they weren't completely bare. She still hadn't moved an inch, but the tension was so thick, John could almost taste it. The hot, metallic bite of it left him wanting more.

He could see her eyes surveying the crowd. When they came to John's table, he could have sworn her gaze locked on his, but he was sure every other man in the crowd felt the very same way. Each man *wanted* to think she was dancing just for him.

The pace of the music built along with the volume. With a measured deliberation, the dancer started to move, almost imperceptibly at first, then minutely faster. After a few seconds her hips were undulating in perfect synchronization with the rhythm. Her shoulders followed, and within seconds, her entire body was moving, slowly, sensually, erotically.

John had been in more strip bars than he cared to remember, but never had he seen a woman dance this way before. It almost seemed as if she *were* the music, moving in perfect harmony with it, the graceful lift of her arms and body a perfect counterpoint to every downbeat, every note, every breath the music took. Watching the action unfold, he could do nothing but stare.

She must have danced for at least five minutes, but it seemed to John that he blinked and it was over. All at once, the lights went out, the music fell silent, and the crowd held its collective breath, stunned and disbelieving. A second later, the stage was empty. The room erupted in wild clapping, cat calls and loud demands for an encore.

Only then did John realize the woman had never disrobed.

Only then did he realize who she was.

CHAPTER SEVEN

TRACY KENSINGTON was waiting in the darkness just past the curtains when Elizabeth dashed backstage. Yanking off her mask, Elizabeth brushed past the other dancer, her knees trembling with equal parts fatigue and fright.

She'd expected to be nervous, but she hadn't been. The music had taken over and the moves had come to her without even the effort of thought. They'd come so easily, in fact, it scared her. Was it so simple to slip back into the life? She'd always told herself she danced for one reason and one reason only—she needed the money. She hadn't enjoyed it as April had. Now she wondered if she'd been lying to herself all those years. Getting up there on stage and letting the music seep into her, she'd been able to put everything behind her and concentrate on nothing but the ebb and flow of her body's motion. It had removed her from her problems.

Until she'd seen John.

Tracy snaked out a hand and stopped Elizabeth's

bolt from the stage. "Hey, you okay? You look kinda pale. Like you seen a ghost or something."

"I—I'm fine," Elizabeth answered, glancing over her shoulder. John was going to appear any moment, she was sure. She had no idea what he would say, but she didn't want him saying it in front of Tracy. She had to maintain her anonymity for as long as she could, or the girls would never tell her anything. She started jogging backward as she spoke. "Just a little out of practice, that's all."

"I don't think so." Tracy's expression was puzzled. "You looked pretty damned good to me."

Elizabeth had expected Tracy to be unfriendly and resentful—Lizzie Bennet was the new girl, after all—but Tracy surprised her. She was not only friendly but helpful. Maybe April hadn't been completely honest when she'd laid the blame on Tracy for all their animosity.

Elizabeth kept going. "Well, uh, thanks…"

Tracy continued to stare at her. "Hey—you sure seem familiar. Haven't we met before?"

Elizabeth's mouth went cottony dry. They had met once, but she hadn't thought Tracy would remember her. Why should she? Any resemblance to April would have been slight, particularly because April had always dyed and permed her hair, while Elizabeth had left hers alone. And the green contacts April usually wore had made the differences in their appearance even greater. But Elizabeth didn't want

Tracy any more suspicious than she obviously already was. She stopped, smiled—and lied. "I don't think so, but I get told that all the time. I think I must look like a lot of people or something."

"No." Tracy shook her head firmly. "No, you look like someone I know, but I just can't figure out who right now. It'll come to me, though. It always does."

A commotion sounded behind the two women, and Elizabeth's pulse began to thump. It had to be John. "I…I gotta run," she said. "We'll talk more later, okay?"

"Sure…" Tracy said, "And maybe I'll remember who you look like."

Praying otherwise, Elizabeth hurried down the narrow hallway heading for the dressing room at the far end. The corridor and everything else backstage was grim and dark and smelled of old beer—a complete contrast to the sections of the club the patrons saw. She was opening the scarred door to the tiny area where the women changed when Greg's voice stopped her. His tone was loud and would clearly brook no argument.

"Lizzie! Wait a minute."

She turned slowly, her mask in her hand, her heart in her throat. The tiny hallway was filled by the two men she least wanted to see. Greg Lansing, who looked clearly unhappy, and John Mallory, whose face was unreadable.

"What's the problem?" She made her voice rough and slightly dismissive. "I've only got a few minutes to change."

Lansing tilted his head at John. "This is Detective Mallory with H.P.D. He says he's got to talk to you. Bob caught him coming backstage."

Bob was the bouncer, a huge ex-wrestler. Elizabeth could only imagine that little scenario. At least John hadn't given her away. Yet.

"I don't know 'im." She turned her back on both men and began to push open the door. But as he'd done in her kitchen, John suddenly materialized beside her.

There was no room to spare in the cramped and darkened hall. His chest took up most of the space, his shoulders the rest. He looked down at her, his eyes flashing, his hand over her trembling fingers still poised on the doorknob. His touch was as hard as his voice, and there was no mistaking his anger. Despite his attitude and appearance—or maybe because of it, she thought with sudden realization—her awareness of him jumped up another notch.

"It's not necessary for you to know me," he growled. "I want to talk with you, and I've got a badge that says you have to—whether you like it or not."

He was keeping up the pretense, but his tone scared her. He meant what he was saying.

Her stare challenged his. "I haven't done anything wrong."

"I didn't say you had."

"Then what's the problem?"

"I think you know what it is, *Madame Leda.*"

She blushed hotly in the darkness, aware of John's closeness but even more aware of Greg Lansing standing in the hall and watching the interchange take place. She glanced at him. Sometime during the confrontation, Tracy had appeared, as well. Greg met Elizabeth's eyes with a narrowed gaze. He was measuring her and measuring the situation. If she didn't act with just the right amount of belligerence, he'd get suspicious. If she responded too aggressively, he'd wonder what she was hiding.

"Do I have to talk to this jerk—"

"Yes." Greg interrupted, his voice brusque. "He won't leave until you do. Just make sure you aren't late for the next set."

Elizabeth looked up at John once more. His face was enigmatic.

"All right," she said curtly, dropping her hand from the knob. "Let's go to the bar out front."

He stepped back as much as he could, and she brushed his chest as she passed him, another spark of something flying between them. She covered up quickly and, wearing a surly expression, stalked to the end of the hall where Tracy and Lansing waited.

She glanced at Tracy, then got her second surprise. There was sympathy in the dancer's green eyes.

John's appearance might actually help her, Elizabeth realized in that second. In Tracy's mind she and Tracy were on the same side—against him. Elizabeth rolled her eyes in mock disgust and Tracy answered with a fed-up look of understanding. With John beside her, Elizabeth reached the front bar a few minutes later, picking a quiet table all the way at the back. Keeping up the deception, John stayed silent until they'd both sat down and given the waitress their drink order. Elizabeth's heart was pounding when the waitress finally left and John turned toward her.

In the smoky darkness of the bar, his gaze moved downward. Her outfit seemed to provide a lot less coverage than it had a moment before. When his eyes returned to her face, she knew she was blushing, something she hadn't done on the stage with a hundred strangers watching. The waitress brought their drinks and disappeared again.

John reached out slowly for his beer, took a sip, then put the bottle back down. He wasn't sure what he wanted to say and he was even less sure of what he was feeling. A mixture of emotions washed over him. Anger. Curiosity. More interest than he wanted to admit to.

His eyes went to Elizabeth's hand. Her fingers were tight on the glass before her, but she hadn't picked it up. It only held soda—no matter what the girls ordered, that's what they got—and he felt a bit sorry for her. She could have used something stronger, he was sure.

The silence between them stretched until he leaned forward, looked into her eyes and said the last thing he intended to say.

"You're very good."

Clearly shocked by the compliment, she stayed mute for a few seconds, then replied, "Thank you."

"You have a real feel for the music."

"Y-yes."

"But I don't think you learned to dance like that at the Harriet Beecham Center for the Performing Arts in Dallas."

She stared at her drink, then back up at him. "No, I didn't."

"Would you like to tell me about it?"

Her dark eyes met his. There was a flicker of pain, a gleam of regret, in their depths before she shook her head. "Not here," she said. "And not now."

He started to press her, then thought better of it. Elizabeth wouldn't respond to that kind of tactic. He'd have to take it easy. He nodded. "Then tell me what you hope to accomplish—" he tilted his head to her outfit "—by doing this."

"I wanted to see if I could get the girls to talk to me. And I need to look in April's locker."

"You couldn't just ask Greg to show you the locker?"

"He'd say no."

"He obviously doesn't know you?"

"That's right. We've never met."

"You don't think you look enough like April to rouse his suspicions?"

"You've seen the photos. With April's dyed and curled hair and contacts you wouldn't think we were sisters, much less twins."

He nodded thoughtfully. "And how long do you plan on doing this?"

"I don't know. As long as it takes, I guess."

"What about your other job?"

"It'll wait. Nothing's more important than finding April, and Betty's explaining that to my clients. My sister is missing and I had to take a personal leave. That's all they need to know."

"Even the rush job you told me about? Masterson?"

"I'm taking care of it by working on the file at home in my spare time."

He looked around the club, then back at her. "You aren't worried someone will recognize you?"

"Not really, especially with the mask." She shrugged. "I don't care one way or the other, though. April's all I care about."

The answer was purely selfless, something he had come to expect from her, but the lack of concern over her own well-being scared him. "And what about you?" He leaned closer to her and spoke over the small table. "This is a dangerous place, Elizabeth."

"I can take care of myself."

"Are you sure?"

"I've been responsible for everyone in my life, including myself, since I was twelve. I think I can handle the Esquire Club."

"And if someone here is behind April's disappearance?"

"Then I'll find out, won't I."

"Before they find out who *you* are?"

"That's the plan."

He paused. "I guess that means you didn't notice Greg Lansing's hand."

"His hand?"

"He's wearing a bandage, Elizabeth."

Her mouth fell open and she was about to respond when the waitress appeared suddenly at their table. She bent down and said something in Elizabeth's ear.

John followed her gaze as she looked toward the other end of the room. In the shadows, behind the bar, Greg Lansing waited, his huge arms crossed, a scowl on his face. "Tell him I'll be right there," Elizabeth said to the waitress.

The waitress nodded, took her tray and left. Elizabeth turned to John. "I didn't see the bandage, but

I can't talk about that right now. I've got to go,'' she said. ''I've got another set coming up and I have to change, too.'' She rose from the table and John stood as well. Stepping in front of her, he put his hand on her arm. Beneath his touch, she tensed.

''I don't like this,'' he said quietly. ''I think you're making a big mistake.''

She looked down at his fingers and once again, he followed her gaze. Her skin was ivory and the contrast of his tanned hand against the alabaster paleness was startling in the dark light of the bar. She'd emphasized the exotic tilt of her eyes with makeup and as she lifted her gaze and stared at him, he couldn't help himself. His body responded…to her look, to her near nakedness, even to the wispy scent of her perfume as it rose between them.

''I'll never learn anything if I stay on the outside, John. This is the only way.''

''No, it's not. I offered to handle this, remember? And you accepted that help. What changed?''

She blinked, the dark sweep of her lashes brushing her high cheekbones before she looked up at him again. ''There are some things you just can't do.''

''Give me some time. You might be surprised.''

''You could have forever, but you'll never be able to make Tracy Kensington trust you or Greg Lansing open up to you. This is something I have to do, John. From the inside.''

His fingers tightened against her arm. She was right, of course. She would have access to information this way, information he'd have no chance in hell of getting. He didn't like it, though, not one damned bit. "Will you call me when you get home?"

"It'll be too late."

"It doesn't matter."

"All right," she said reluctantly after a moment. "I guess I can call."

"I'll be waiting," he said, his gaze pinning hers. "Don't forget."

ELIZABETH DID TWO more sets. John watched the second one, but when she came out on the darkened stage for the last time she couldn't find him. From behind the mask, she searched the smoke-filled dimness of the audience as she moved to the music, but she didn't see him. Relief washed over her, then right on its heels came disappointment. The realization shocked her. Did she want John watching her do this?

Or did she just want John?

Pushing the questions to the very back of her mind, Elizabeth returned to the dressing room and marveled again at how easy it was to get back into the life. When she was younger and had danced, she would walk out on stage, put her mind on hold and simply move to the music. She never really saw the customers, never heard the calls or whistles. She danced, and in her mind, she went to a private place. A lot of times when the music finished, she was surprised. April had teased her about this, then one day Elizabeth had explained.

"It's easy for you," she'd said. "You're gorgeous and you enjoy all the attention. It's a means to an end for me. Nothing more."

April had lifted one eyebrow. "Oh, c'mon. You don't like it? Knowing there's a hundred men out there watching you, wondering about you, thinking just about you... That isn't a turn-on for you?"

"No," Elizabeth had answered quickly. "I'm doing it for the money...for us and for Mom. That's all."

April had looked at her for just a moment in that knowing way she had. It was something about the way she tilted her head. "You like it," she'd said without hesitation. "You just can't admit it. It doesn't go with the image you've got of yourself— the one you carry inside your head." She'd paused then smiled the smile that matched the tilt of her head. "Trust me, Elizabeth. You like it...you just can't accept that you do."

Elizabeth had hotly denied April's pronouncement.

But now she wondered.

Once inside the dressing room, Elizabeth reapplied her makeup then reached into her locker for

her street clothes, chatting with the few other dancers that had worked equally late. As she stepped into
her jeans then slipped her arms into her blouse, she
wondered how she could bring up April's name. Her
fingers stilled on her buttons as she tried to decide
how to approach the subject, then the outer door
opened, and Greg Lansing stood on the threshold.

In the chipped and cloudy mirrors surrounding
the makeup tables, Elizabeth's startled gaze caught
his eyes. At the very last second she stopped herself
from grabbing the placket of her blouse and closing
it. She reminded herself he'd definitely seen her
wearing less, and she left the shirt hanging open.

Ignoring the other women, he came directly to her
and stopped beside her locker. In the tiny, crowded
dressing room, filled with the scent of a dozen different perfumes and the heat of the dancers' bodies,
he loomed over her, his blue eyes cold and narrow.
She felt hot, almost ill, and even though she knew
she should meet his stare, she couldn't, not with her
stomach rolling around in fear. She dropped her
gaze to the buttons of her blouse.

And that's when she saw Greg's right hand. John
had been right. A huge, flesh colored bandage covered most of the skin. It was big enough to conceal
almost any kind of injury...including a tangle with
a knife.

She flashed on the dark figure of a man beside a
broken window, a gloved hand, a covered face.

"What happened?" She spoke boldly, but her heart was lodged in her throat, making it tough to speak. "Get into something you shouldn't have?"

He grimaced and looked down at the gauze, dropping his hold on his wounded fingers as if embarrassed to have been caught protecting them. "It's nothing," he answered. "A run-in with the ice machine out back." He switched topics abruptly. "What'd that detective want with you? You aren't in any kind of trouble with the law, are you? I operate a clean place here."

A run-in with an ice machine? Elizabeth stared at him, her mind whirling as she struggled to focus on the question Greg had asked. "The cop? He's working the Strip. Looking for some woman who disappeared." She finished buttoning her blouse and bent down to tie her shoes. "He thought I might have been at some of the other clubs and heard something. I told him I didn't know her. I been dancing in Dallas. I don't know anyone from around here."

"That's not true. You know us now."

Elizabeth looked up. Tracy stood beside Greg and she was smiling in such a friendly fashion Elizabeth immediately felt guilty. "Besides, that Mallory guy's a pain in the ass," she went on. "He's talking to all the girls, Greg. You need to do something about him."

"He's a cop, Tracy. I can't *do* anything about him."

"He's harassing us."

"Don't you want to find poor April?"

Elizabeth kept her head down.

"Oh, yeah, I'm dying to find April. You know that, don't you, Greg?"

He made a sound of disgust, turned on his heel and left. The door banged shut behind him, and Tracy peeled off what was left of her costume. Which was little.

One of the women behind Elizabeth spoke. "*Has* anyone heard anything about April?"

Elizabeth held her breath.

"*I* haven't," Tracy answered, "and if I don't, I won't be crying in my beer, either."

"Who is this chick?" Elizabeth asked, her face hidden behind her locker door.

Tracy explained quickly.

"And she just disappeared?"

"That's right. Can't say that my heart is breakin'."

A locker door slammed shut, and a statuesque brunette walked up to Tracy. She had hazel eyes, a full mane of hair and a body that made men weep. Elizabeth had seen their reaction. She'd been on right before Elizabeth. "Does that mean you gonna try and lasso Greg again?"

Tracy looked at the woman. "Yes, it does,

Brownie, so you can keep your acrylic claws away from him. And for your information, I don't need to 'lasso' him. He was in my bed last night.''

The woman held up her palms. ''He's all yours, honey. I don't want nothin' to do with the man. Just askin', that's all.'' She walked away, her heels clicking on the bare concrete floor as she opened the outer door and left.

Elizabeth closed her locker. She wore tinted glasses she didn't need and had painted her lips crimson. She hardly recognized herself; she didn't think Tracy could possibly link her to her sister. She pointed to April's locker. ''This the one who's gone?''

''That's hers.''

On impulse, Elizabeth reached out to the metal cabinet and gave the handle a swift jerk. She hadn't needed to worry about a lock. Ever since one of the girls had hidden a gun in her locker, Greg had insisted on having free access. The door opened with a screech and, pulse hammering, Elizabeth leaned forward and looked inside.

It was empty.

Hiding her disappointment, she slammed the door shut under Tracy's curious gaze. ''What do you think happened?'' Elizabeth asked nonchalantly.

''Who knows?'' Tracy pulled a red T-shirt over her bare chest, then glanced behind her before speaking again. "With April, it coulda been anything. She had a way of finding trouble."

"Yeah. Some women are like that." Elizabeth's pulse sputtered into a faster pace, but she made her voice casual.

"April was worse than most. She'd go out looking for it if it didn't come to her."

"Like the deal with Lansing?"

Tracy's head jerked up and her gaze filled with suspicion. "Wh-what do you mean? What deal with Lansing?"

"Well, she took him from you, didn't she? Isn't that what you said to the other girl—Brownie?"

Tracy's expression cleared, and all Elizabeth could do was stare. What had Tracy thought she'd meant? Clearly there was something else going on, but what?

"Oh…yeah, that. She did—but I knew it wouldn't last. Greg and I go back a long way. He might stray every once in a while, but he usually wanders on home." Her mouth formed a hard line and her eyes narrowed. It was not an attractive expression and it added five years to her face. "Why are *you* so interested?"

Elizabeth held up her hands just as Brownie had and shook her head. "Hey, he's a good lookin' dude, right? What woman wouldn't want to know the lay of the land?"

Tracy stared at her for a second, then smiled.

"Yeah, well, he is a looker, but believe me, if April couldn't handle him, you can't, either."

A thousand questions sprang into Elizabeth's mind, but she had to ignore them. Any more and Tracy's suspicions would grow. Elizabeth changed the subject to the first thing she could think of.

"That Mallory guy," she said brightly. "A real jerk, huh?"

Tracy hesitated, then let herself be diverted. "Yeah, he's trouble all right, but there's something about him..."

Digging in her purse for her car keys, Elizabeth paused. "Whaddaya mean?"

"I don't know...something about him makes you feel different inside, you know? And *he's* different, too. I mean he's a cop and everything, but he's not like most of the assholes you see around here. I don't know what it is, but he makes me wish..." Her voice died as she stared into the dim confines of the almost empty dressing room.

"That things were different," Elizabeth supplied flatly.

Tracy's emerald gaze slowly shifted and focused on her. "Yeah," she said quietly, nodding her head. "I think that's exactly what I mean. He's a straight arrow. One of those guys your mama would love. 'Course, if she knew what he did to you in the bedroom..." She finished pulling on her boots and stood. "That kinda guy doesn't bother with women like us, though. He might look, might even do a little more than that, but he'd want Donna Reed at home, you can bet on it."

Elizabeth did the only thing she could. She agreed. Then she said good-night, turned around and left, Tracy's words echoing in her mind.

CHAPTER EIGHT

JOHN PICKED UP the phone on the first ring. He was standing by the window and had seen Elizabeth's lights come on. "Hello?"

"It's me. I'm home." Elizabeth sounded weary, but behind the exhaustion, John heard something else. The wary guardedness she'd put between them the first few times they'd spoken had returned and he understood exactly why.

He now knew one of her secrets.

"How'd it go?" he asked, keeping his voice casual. "Hear anything interesting from anyone?"

She hesitated just a second, then spoke. "Tracy did say something I found intriguing."

John didn't wait for her to say more or to give him permission. "I'm coming over. Put on a pot of coffee."

Two minutes later he was standing on the small porch outside Elizabeth's front door. She opened it before he could knock, then stepped aside for him to enter. He brushed past her, reminding himself of the moment in the hallway when he'd seen her earlier this evening. He'd felt something jump between them and so had she. He knew it. Now, looking down into that same dark gaze, John felt it again. A velvet rope winding around them both and pulling them closer and closer, whether they liked it or not.

"You didn't need to come over." She closed the door behind him. "I could have told you everything on the phone."

She wore a robe, and not the thick terry-cloth thing she'd put on the night after she'd been at April's. No, this was white silk and thin with a delicate tracery of flowers stretching across one shoulder and arcing down the back. It covered her much more completely than the outfit she'd danced in, but now he knew a lot more about the body beneath the garment. John felt the heat of his response before he could curb it.

"I wanted to see you," he said. "I wanted to make sure you were all right."

Reluctantly, it seemed, she tilted her head toward her living room. "Come inside and sit down, then. The coffee's almost ready—I had a pot already started. I'll go get it."

John walked into her living room and found himself staring at the photograph on the mantel, the one he'd looked at before. This time he studied it more closely, but he really didn't have to. He had his answer. The other photo, the one locked in his desk that April Benoit had had hidden in her apartment was of April and Elizabeth. He knew that now.

The two girls here, dressed in their ballet finery, stared back at the camera. April confronted the lens, but Elizabeth had a...dreamy look in her eyes. He guessed that mentally she was nowhere near the stage or the ballet. She'd worn the same expression this evening.

She came up behind him and handed him a mug, sending a glance of her own toward the photograph. "I suppose you're wondering how we went from *Swan Lake* to the Esquire Club."

He took the coffee mug and nodded. "It does seem to be a jump, but I assume there's a good reason."

Her expression didn't change, but the steam from her coffee mug rose to drift in front of her face. For a second she seemed to waver, but only because of the wisp of steam. "You could say that. It's called survival."

"Tell me what happened."

She looked at him over the rim of the mug. "You don't really want to know. It's not important, anyway."

She turned and started to move away, but John reached out and stopped her with a hand on her shoulder. Underneath the silk her skin felt hot, almost feverish. "I don't ask questions if I don't want answers."

She shrugged carelessly, and that was when he understood. She was embarrassed, ashamed. Whatever had started her and her sister down the path they'd taken was something Elizabeth Benoit had worked hard to put behind her. The business suits, the tight bun of hair, her remote air—all props to defend her against exposure.

God, how much she must love April to drop all that armor!

"There's nothing you can say that would shock me, Elizabeth. I've heard it all, believe me."

She walked toward the window. "I know. And that's what's so tawdry about it. There's nothing unique or particularly interesting about what happened to us. It just happened…and we did the best we could."

John crossed to where she stood, his coffee mug still in his hand. She must have taken a quick shower before she'd called him. The faint scent of shampoo from the shining mass of her hair met his nostrils. They stood silently by the window. Finally she spoke.

"We grew up in Dallas—a fairy-tale life. More money than we could spend, a beautiful home, servants, clothes—everything. My mother had no… balance in her life, but that only made my father love her more. They were so crazy about each other that April and I almost felt left out sometimes. But I thought everything was perfect. Then one day, when we were twelve years old, I went outside into the garage to look for my parents." Her face took on a calm, but somehow more remote expression. "I found my father. Dead. He'd been shot."

"Shit…" John breathed the word out slowly. He didn't know what he'd expected to hear, but this wasn't it.

"My mother was there. I'll never forget how she was just sitting on the floor, looking at him." Elizabeth lifted her eyes to his face. "The gun was lying on the floor between them."

"Was it suicide or…?"

"I don't know. We could never figure it out. And in the confusion afterward, the truth hardly seemed to matter."

"Was there an investigation?"

"Oh, yes, it was looked into."

"They should have found residue…"

"They'd been target practicing earlier and both of them had been shooting."

"But there's splatter patterns and gunpowder burns and—"

Elizabeth stopped him by holding up her hand. "John, I was only a kid when it happened. The officials in charge told me they couldn't tell exactly what had occurred, and I believed them because I didn't have another choice." She shrugged. "Maybe they knew and wanted to protect us. Either way, by the time I was old enough to wonder, it didn't seem to matter much."

"Why not?"

"Dad had gotten into our trust funds, the ones his parents had set up for us, their grandchildren. He'd apparently been on the edge for some time and had kept it from all of us, even my mom. Not that she would have held it against him. She absolutely adored him. She looked at Daddy as a god, almost."

"So your finances changed..."

"No. You don't understand." She waited until his eyes met hers again. "There was *no* money. Absolutely nothing. The checking account was overdrawn, the savings accounts were empty. He hadn't paid the mortgage in so many months they'd already started foreclosure proceedings against the house. The day after he died, there were men with tow trucks removing the cars from that same garage."

"What went wrong?" he asked. "Bad business deal, stock market gone south? What?"

"My father gambled," she said quietly. "On anything and everything. None of us knew about it, not even my mother. He had five bookies and he owed each of them more money than you and I could ever make in a dozen lifetimes. He'd been juggling his debts and loans for years, but finally it all came tumbling down."

There was a beat of silence before she spoke again. He had a strong feeling she'd never told anyone what she was telling him now. She swallowed hard. "I've always suspected he told Mom about the money and she shot him. She was probably just trying to scare him by waving the gun at him or something. She wasn't violent and wouldn't have wanted to kill him, but they would fight like crazy sometimes. She was incredibly unstable. She'd fly off the handle in an instant and yell and scream at him, then she'd apologize and beg forgiveness and they'd be in love all over again.'' Elizabeth stared down at her hands, then back up at John. ''In the end, it didn't matter how he died, one way or the other. She put herself in her own prison after that.''

''What do you mean?''

''She lost her mind. Became completely unhinged. There was nothing to do but put her in a state facility. April and I moved from foster home to foster home because we didn't have any other relatives.''

John stood quietly, knowing there was nothing he could say. Her face was expressionless, and he could only imagine the pain she'd gone through. He thought of the two little girls in April's photograph. It was one thing to grow up poor, but to become that way overnight just because your father couldn't control a habit? John had been a cop long enough to see what happened to kids in foster homes. Some of the substitute parents were saints—but others weren't.

As if she'd read his mind, she spoke again, her voice husky. ''We hated the homes. They were really bad. Sometimes they had to split us up and that

was even worse. Two young girls, pretty, innocent...'' Her eyes were distant. ''You can fill in the
blanks. Needless to say we got out as soon as we
were old enough. We took the first jobs we could
find.''

''Dancing?''

''No...waitressing. At a pancake house. It was
the only thing we could do without any experience.
I worked double shifts and so did April.'' She shook
her head. ''Four years before, we shopped only at
Neiman-Marcus. Now we were counting our tips
and sneaking food off plates to take home later.''

John couldn't stop himself. He reached out and
put his hand on her back. He thought he'd seen her
tremble, but the movement came and went so
quickly he wasn't sure. His fingers squeezed her
shoulder with reassurance, but it seemed to be a
useless gesture.

''We'd been working for three months when a
guy came in one night. His name was Donnie Bar-
ker. I was busy in the kitchen. He took one look at
April and handed her his card. 'When you get tired
of working for a living, come see me, doll,' he said.
'If you've got the body under that uniform I think
you do, I can get you $500 a night in tips. At least.'
He thought he'd died and gone to heaven—that's
how April put it—when she told him she had a twin.

''April wanted to quit that night. She cornered me
by the coffeepot and begged me to go with her to

his club after our shift.'' Elizabeth shook her head. ''We went, still dressed for work. We didn't have the money for the cover charge but the guy at the door understood the minute he saw us. Donnie recruited girls like us all the time.''

''Was it hard? To work there at the club?''

''Oh, I didn't do it. Not at first.'' Her words became bitter. ''We compromised. She went to work at the club as a waitress. I stayed at the pancake house.''

''But...''

Her eyes went back to the window and the inky night beyond. ''But April couldn't resist. She saw how much more the dancers made than the cocktail waitresses and she started dancing. It wasn't really the money. She just wanted to be able to afford the life we'd had before—a family, a home, stability. That was impossible, of course, but she didn't understand it and I didn't discourage her. We moved into an apartment we didn't have to share with roaches the size of rats and we could actually afford a hamburger out once a month. Things got better for us—a fact April reminded me of just before she disappeared.''

Elizabeth stopped and cleared her throat. ''Then the state hospital said they had to cut back. We could either move Mom into a private facility or they'd put her out on the street. We found her a place, but it was incredibly expensive. The same week, April got sick. I had to take her to the emergency room and she had to have her appendix removed. By the time it was all over, we had nothing. No money at all. We were going to be homeless. So I went to the club and started dancing. When April recovered, she came back and we started an act together.'' Her voice cracked. ''It seemed as if it was the only choice at the time.''

''It was.''

She stepped away from the window and away from him. Moving to the couch, she sat down heavily. ''I'm not so sure now. It's taken April from me. There had to have been some other way.''

''You got out. She could have, too.''

Elizabeth shook her head. ''That's what I was telling her the night we fought. Anyway, after four years in the private facility, Mom had a heart attack and died. Our expenses eased up and I started taking some economics classes at the University of Dallas. I saw how the older dancers fared and I wasn't going to put myself through that. Not after everything else. I tried to get April to go with me, but she wouldn't.''

He didn't know what to do or what to say. She'd reject any kind of sympathy, and expressing anything else just didn't seem right. He could tell her how amazed he was at what she'd done with herself—how much he admired her strength and the love she had for her family—but he didn't really have the right words to express it all. He waited a moment, then asked quietly, "What did Tracy say tonight, Elizabeth?"

She roused herself and shook her head. "It...it wasn't what she said as much as what she *didn't* say—about Lansing. I asked about the deal between April and him, and Tracy got really nervous. I explained that I meant their relationship, and she relaxed, but I sensed there's something there. Something beyond the obvious...."

"Did you get a chance to look in April's locker?"

"Yeah. It was completely empty." She looked up. "But I saw Lansing's hand."

John crossed to her and sank down beside her. "He said he cut it on the ice machine. I talked to the bartender, and he confirmed the story, but who knows if he's telling the truth."

"Damn. I'd almost convinced myself that was him at April's apartment."

"Why?"

"I don't know," she answered, her voice full of frustration. "Because I wanted a direction to look in, I guess. And because of what you said, too. You know, about how most victims know their assailants?"

"Lansing was working the night April disappeared, Elizabeth. That was one of the first things I checked."

"He could have been lying."

John nodded. "He could have—if I'd asked him. I talked to one of the hostesses, though. She told me he never left the building that night. It's entirely possible she could be covering for him, probably is, but I have to hear the excuses before I can disprove them."

Agitated suddenly, Elizabeth jumped to her feet. "Of course she's lying! These people do that first and tell the truth second. Greg's probably told them to say he's working every night whether he is or not."

"Elizabeth, I worked Vice. I know these kinds of people even better than you do." John also rose from the couch. "But I have to investigate, ask questions, get answers, even if they are lies. I have to *prove* him guilty, not just assume that's the case."

"Oh, he's guilty, all right. I'm positive."

"And it's my job to make sure the D.A. will agree with you. But the only way I can do that is by asking the questions."

"I know that!" Much the same as the first time they'd talked, her dark eyes filled suddenly with tears, the instant flood of emotion surprising him. "It's just that…that I'm scared my sister's dead and she's the only person I have left in the world I give a damn about…and wh-who gives a damn about me, too."

In an instant John crossed the space between

them. Her eyes were huge and she was definitely trembling now. He did the only thing he could. He reached out for her and pulled her toward him.

She wavered for just a second, taut and tense in the circle of his embrace, then all at once, she seemed to melt, her body collapsing. John caught her as much as anything else, his arms going around her and bringing her to his chest.

Even though her body was supple and strong, she felt less…substantial than he'd expected. Lighter somehow, almost fragile. She quivered against him for a moment, then tilted back her head to look at him.

The naked expression in her gaze stole his breath and stopped his heart. It was so needy, so clearly wanting all he had to give that he didn't know what to do. He looked at her and only one thought shot into his head with clarity. He had to take care of this woman, this woman who thought she needed no one.

Without thinking further, he bent down and kissed her.

ELIZABETH DIDN'T RESIST. She surrendered to John's kiss and for a moment, she let herself feel nothing but the warmth of his arms and the hard pressure of his lips. When he pressed against her closer and nudged her mouth open with his own, she gave in to that, too. From the back of her mind came Tracy's words: *"One of those guys your mama would love. 'Course, if she knew what he did to you in the bedroom...."*

His hands were strong against the small of her back, his chest solid beneath her breasts. Her already fast pulse quickened even more as he murmured her name into her open mouth. She knew she should pull back, should move out of his heated embrace and away from the refuge he offered, but she couldn't. It had been too long since she'd allowed a man to hold her this way, since she'd forfeited all control and let her emotions rule instead of her brain. She couldn't have pushed him away if her life had depended on it.

So she did the only thing she could. She gave in and let it happen. She'd find herself wondering, later that night, where it might have led if John's beeper hadn't gone off.

His brown eyes still locked with hers, he leaned away from her, his hand going to his waistband and the insistently buzzing device. His gaze held frustration and more than just a little irritation, but overlaying each emotion was something else. She recognized it, because the same thing was shivering down her spine. Desire. A hot, almost liquid kind of need that could be satisfied by only one thing. Her legs went weak as he cursed softly and broke their gaze to look at the number flashing on the beeper.

The next thing she knew, he was heading for the kitchen—the phone, she presumed—without a backward glance. She sank onto the sofa beside her.

Dazed and frightened at the strength of her reaction to his caresses, Elizabeth listened with half an ear to John's muffled one-way conversation.

"Uh-huh. Okay? When did they find it?"

Silence stretched.

"A lot of it? All right. Get the CSU guys on it. I'll get what I need from this end and meet you there in twenty."

She heard the phone click back into its cradle, then John's boots as they thudded across the floor of the kitchen, the hallway, then reentered the living room. She turned on the couch to look at him, her heart sinking when she saw his expression.

"Wh-what is it?" she asked, rising. "What's wrong?"

He moved around the sofa and came up to her. "They've found your car, Elizabeth. Down on Dowling Street."

Her heart sank further. "April...?"

He shook his head. "Just the car."

"On Dowling? Oh, God..." It was the worst part of downtown Houston. Her stomach joined her heart, on the floor, by her feet. "What in the world would she be doing down there?" she said with dismay.

"Just because the car was there, it doesn't mean *she* was."

Elizabeth stared at him, her expression shifting as his meaning finally became clear. "Oh, God..."

He closed the space between them and grasped her shoulders, his fingers digging into the skin with an almost painful intensity. "Elizabeth...I've got to go. I want to check this out, look at your car." His gaze swept her face. "I don't usually kiss a woman, then run out the door..."

With the memory of his lips still fresh, she looked into his eyes and shook her head. "You're not running out the door this time, either. I've got to know what's happening, too. I'm going with you."

THERE WAS STILL traffic on the freeway, even at three in the morning. Speeding along Highway 59 toward downtown, John glanced across the seat of the pickup at Elizabeth. She'd changed into jeans and a T-shirt and was pressed against the door, a mixture of hope and anxiety marring her beautiful face.

She was going to be even more miserable when they got to Dowling. He'd tried to argue with her, tried to get her to stay at home, but his words had fallen on deaf ears. For the first time, he'd seen some of what had gotten her so far. Stubbornness, determination—he didn't know what to call it, but he knew she had it.

They reached the exit a few minutes later, the flashing blue and red lights leading John the rest of the way. He pulled up behind the city tow truck, which was already poised to take the Mercedes down to the lab.

Elizabeth bounded out before he could stop her. Before he could warn her.

Throwing open his door, John jumped out and followed her, but too late. In seconds Elizabeth reached the car and before any of the other cops could stop her, she'd yanked open the door and looked inside. John groaned, but he also understood. Even though he'd told her there was no sign of April, she wanted to see for herself.

And see she would. Because he'd lied. There *were* signs *someone* had been in the car. There was blood on the front seat.

Holding on to the roof of the car, Elizabeth swayed, then looked up as John reached her side. Her face was drained of color and her skin glowed bonelike in the eerie beams of light. One of the nearby officers, a rookie John recognized, got to the opened door at the same time as John.

"Miss, you can't be here. Please…this is a crime scene…"

"It's okay, McGaffey." John took Elizabeth's arm and she sagged against him. "This is Ms. Benoit. The car belongs to her. I'll handle it."

The rookie took one look at Elizabeth's ashen

face, then nodded. "Oh…right. Okay." He backed away, clearly more than happy to let John take care of the situation.

Elizabeth glanced toward the car again, a strangled sound coming from somewhere in the back of her throat. "Th-that's blood, isn't it? The hand print…"

He shot a glance into the car. On the leather seat, as clearly outlined as a child's drawing, was the smudged shape of a hand. Drawn in blood. He nodded.

She lifted a shaky hand to push back a strand of hair that had fallen into her eyes. "That's why you didn't want me coming here."

"Now, Elizabeth, we don't know for sure that it's April's," he said.

She looked back inside and spoke, almost as if to herself. "It's hers. I can tell it's hers. I have a bad feeling about this.…"

He took her arm and steered her off to one side. McGaffey's partner, an older cop named Anderson, came up to them. He nodded to John, but focused on Elizabeth. "This is your automobile, ma'am?"

She nodded weakly.

"Was it stolen?"

John interrupted to explain, the older cop nodding and taking notes. He finally looked up. "Any leads on the sister?"

John shook his head. "Nothing so far."

"We'll need her blood type."

"It's A positive." Elizabeth answered, her voice high and tremulous. "Same as mine."

Anderson glanced sympathetically at her, then at John. Closing his notebook, he angled his head away from where they stood. John understood immediately and turned to Elizabeth. "Why don't you go wait in the car? I'll be right there."

"No." She shook her head, then looked at Anderson. "This is my sister we're talking about. I want to know everything."

Anderson hesitated, then nodded grimly. "Well, there's more blood in the trunk. The CSU guys also got fibers from a blanket or something like that—nothing from the car itself. There was a roll of silver duct tape and—" he looked down at his notes "—one ladies' shoe, black leather, size 6."

"Show me the shoe," Elizabeth said.

The officer glanced again at John. He shrugged, then called to someone behind him. A moment later, he was handed a plastic bag. He held it up for Elizabeth to look at.

John wouldn't have thought it possible for her to go paler, but she did. "Th-that's my shoe. I noticed they were missing last week, but I thought I might have dropped them at the repair shop along with some others I'd taken in. I...I hadn't had time to check."

"Could you have left it in the car?"

"No. I wouldn't have done that." She shook her head, almost apologetically. "I'm particular about my shoes. I always clean them after I wear them and I keep them in special plastic boxes, one for each pair."

"Did you let April borrow your clothes?"

"She took what she wanted to," Elizabeth answered. "But she'd never borrow those...." Her eyes went back to the trunk of the car, then she raised her gaze to the officer. "Tell me what this means."

"It's hard to say, ma'am...."

Her voice was sharp. "Just tell me."

"Well, it looks as if they might have done something to her to get her into the car—struck her probably—then at some point they forced her out of the vehicle and into the trunk. She might have lost the shoe then. Afterward, well, they brought the car here."

Elizabeth looked at John. "Do you agree?"

"It sounds plausible." John glanced up and took in the neighborhood. "The hubcaps and the radio are gone. Wonder how long it's been here?"

"We're asking around, but the local citizens aren't too open to discussion." Anderson nodded toward McGaffey. The rookie was talking to a man dressed in several layers of tattered clothing. Leaning against a shopping cart filled with cans, newspapers and an empty cardboard box, he was shaking his head wildly.

They stared in silence at the man, then John sighed heavily. "Get CSU to dust the car top to bottom. Call me when it's done."

CHAPTER NINE

THE FOLLOWING WEEK Elizabeth functioned as if in a trance. She merely went through the motions of living. She ate, she slept, she danced, and when she wasn't doing any of those, she worked on Linda Tremont's case, the older woman never failing to ask Elizabeth if she'd heard from April and what progress the police had made. But the fog of disbelief and fear Elizabeth lived in wasn't really penetrated by anything other than phone calls to John for updates.

April *couldn't* be dead. She just couldn't. She and Elizabeth were very different in personality, but they shared a strong emotional bond, almost psychic when they'd been younger, and if she was dead now, Elizabeth would *know*. The police report on the blood sample, however, had been positive. The blood type was identical to Elizabeth's. DNA tests were being done to confirm the findings further.

After talking to Linda Tremont one evening and listening to her speak about her brother, for the first time since April had disappeared, Elizabeth forced herself to wonder what it would be like if April *didn't* come back. If the worst had happened. Only one thought came to Elizabeth that managed to stay in focus—and it was the same thought she'd had before. Who would she be if she wasn't April's sister? Who would she be if she didn't have April to care for? Funny—Elizabeth had resented the task and now all she wanted was to have it back.

On Saturday night she stepped on the stage to the sound of throbbing music. For the first time since last week, her mind released her problems—the dancers who wouldn't talk to her, the image of her car, even the bloodstained upholstery. Everything. The throaty sound of Deborah Harry's voice poured out of the speakers and seeped into Elizabeth's psyche, washing away her thoughts and replacing them with a blanket whiteness. The release felt so good, Elizabeth experienced a flicker of guilt. She quickly pushed that emotion aside too, though, and allowed the music to help her.

But her mind couldn't handle the emptiness, and behind the mask she wore, the only other subject she'd been able to think about returned. John Mallory. His face filled her brain, and the memory of his mouth and his hands and his body came with it.

He was the kind of guy who got under your skin. In the least expected moment, she'd think about him, remember something about him—like how his hair curled on the back of his neck, or that scar near his temple. Or the way the pad of his thumb had felt as it smoothed over her jaw when they'd kissed. She remembered, too, the way her body had responded to his. Yes, he was good-looking. Yes, when he gazed into her eyes, he made her feel as if she was the only thing he ever thought about. But the deep-down visceral reaction that had rippled over her...she'd never expected to feel that. Never.

God, she didn't need this kind of confusion. Especially not now. Those years ago when she'd been dating Jack and he'd said the word *marriage,* she'd decided she didn't want that in her life. Now here John was, inching his way into her mind and refusing to leave. It scared her. She'd just have to make sure that kiss was not repeated. He *was* the kind of man Tracy had described, and even if she'd wanted to be, Elizabeth wasn't the kind of woman he really wanted.

The thought brought her full circle back to April. If only she was here! Elizabeth had never trusted her sister's advice about men—about anything, for that matter—but suddenly she wanted nothing as much as she wanted to sit down with April and pour out her heart.

But it might be too late for that.

The music died and so did Elizabeth's movements. When the stage went completely dark, she slipped to the back and headed down the dim hallway, her confusion and anxiety growing.

And that was when she saw him.

Stepping out from one of the side rooms, the man appeared without warning right in front of Elizabeth. She gasped, but the sound was swallowed by the music playing for the next dancer, already on stage.

He was close enough to hear, however, and he lifted one leather-gloved hand, pressing a finger to his lips. "Don't be afraid." He spoke in a perfectly normal voice, but underneath the normalcy there was something else, a chill that Elizabeth immediately sensed...all the way to her bones. "I'm not here to hurt you."

She looked around, but the corridor was empty. "How'd you get back here? Customers aren't allowed—"

"Oh, I'm more than a customer." He smiled and the skin of his face stretched tightly over his cheekbones. "Much, much more." She couldn't guess his age. His hair could have been blond or gray, and the body under the tailored black suit could have been trim or not. But she was sure about one thing. He gave her the creeps. She shivered.

"I don't know who you are and I don't care," she said with a show of bravado. "Just get out of my way. Let me pass or I'm calling Bob."

"Bob?" He remained blocking her way. "Bob wouldn't touch me, my dear. You see, I'm his employer." He waited a beat. "Just as I'm yours."

Elizabeth stood perfectly still, her pulse pounding in her ears.

He extended his hand. "Lyndon Kersh, at your service, Madame Leda..."

She ignored the gloved fingers in front of her, a dim recollection coming to her. April had told her once that the guy who owned the club was a little "strange." Lyndon Kersh went beyond that description in Elizabeth's opinion, but she continued to act as if she didn't know him.

"I work for Greg Lansing," Elizabeth replied.

"And Greg Lansing works for me." He arched one pale eyebrow. "You didn't think Mr. Lansing was the owner of this establishment, did you?"

"I...I didn't really think about it at all."

"Well, you should have. We can't be too careful these days. You never know what might happen."

He blinked and smiled, and for the first time, she noticed his eyes. They were two pale flames, not blue, not green, but a color she'd never seen before. As creepy as the rest of him. Elizabeth shivered again. She grabbed the lapels of her robe and pulled them closer, keeping her hands up protectively.

"Look, Mr. Kersh. I don't know if you're who you say you are or not, but I'd like to pass, please."

He didn't move. "You look frightened. Are you?"

"No. Of course not." She met his chilly stare and

lied boldly. "But I need to get to the dressing room. My shift is over and I want to leave."

"Your eyes are way too big to be telling the truth." He leaned closer. "Have the other dancers been scaring you? Did they tell you about April?"

Elizabeth froze. The walls of the already cramped hallway seemed to move in closer. "Y-you knew April?"

He smiled again. "Oh, the past tense! Do you think April is gone?"

"I've never met her. That's why I used that tense." She licked her bone-dry lips. "But to answer your question, yes. The other dancers have mentioned her."

His expression altered slightly. In the dim light of the corridor she couldn't read it exactly, but his interest was clearly piqued. "Really? What did they say?"

"That she'd disappeared. That no one knows where she is."

"And why do they think this happened?"

"They haven't said."

"Not even the nosy Miss Kensington? She seems to know everything around here."

Would he tell her more if she lied? Elizabeth stared into his pale eyes, but Tracy's face came into her mind and Elizabeth couldn't make herself lie. Beneath the attitude and the cattiness, there was something weak about Tracy. She wouldn't be able to stand up to this man, Elizabeth thought suddenly.

"Tracy's too busy taking care of Lansing," Elizabeth said. "She doesn't have time to spread gossip."

"Oh, really?" He adjusted one of his gloves. "That's not the way I understand it. In fact, Mr. Lansing has told me—"

"Mr. Kersh!"

Elizabeth whirled at the sound of Greg's voice behind her. He stared at her a moment, then switched his gaze to the man in front of her. "I didn't know you were coming down tonight. It's going to take me a minute to get your table ready."

The man in black waved a hand in Elizabeth's direction. "I'm in no hurry, Greg. Madame Leda has been entertaining me. In fact, I've actually been in the audience for a while, watching her act. It's quite unique."

A shiver of unease rippled down Elizabeth's back.

He raised his hand and tapped his chin in a thoughtful manner. "Although, it does remind me of a duo I saw dance in Dallas once." He shifted his bright eyes to Elizabeth. "You wouldn't know anything about them, would you? I think they were twins actually. As is the missing Miss April."

Elizabeth's stomach roiled. She swallowed twice,

then spoke, her voice as cold as she could make it. "I have no idea what you're talking about."

He looked into her eyes. "Don't you?"

"No." She gathered the chiffon around her even more closely and started to move. "So if you'll excuse me…"

Without a word the man stepped to one side, and Elizabeth swept past him. She could feel his eyes burning into her back all the way to the dressing-room door.

JOHN STOOD in the shadow of the doorway just outside Lisa's room. Marsha had actually called and asked him to take her Saturday night, and he couldn't believe his luck. She'd been halfway decent, too, when he'd zoomed over to the house and got Lisa. He was tempted to be suspicious of her motives. She probably wanted something from him, but he wasn't going to worry about that. Not now. He watched his daughter sleep and let his mind return to the topic he'd been obsessed with since last week.

Kissing Elizabeth.

He'd tried to resist, he really had, but what man in his right mind could have looked into those eyes and not given in? She'd needed comfort and reassurance, and putting his arms around her had seemed to be the only way to give her those two things.

C'mon, Mallory! Who're you trying to kid?

With a snort of disgust, he turned and went to the den, crossing to a small desk in one corner. Concentrate on work, he told himself. Stay busy. Keep occupied. She doesn't want you in her life and you don't need her in yours. He stared at the folders of some of his other cases and worked on them for a while, but in the end, when he picked up the phone and dialed the lab, it was to ask about one case and one case only.

The tech told John exactly what he'd expected to hear.

"It's her blood, all right. We sampled the upholstery and the blood in the trunk, too. The DNA matches the sister's DNA perfectly."

"Fingerprints?"

"Surprisingly few. Most of the ones we got correspond to the owner of the car, the rest were only partials at best. Whoever was in the vehicle last must have worn gloves."

"And the handprint?"

"Too smeared to be worth anything. I think that's why they left it."

"What about the fibers?"

"They're a cotton blend. Real typical. Could be a blanket, something like that. I've got a guy working on it some more, but I'm pretty sure they're nothing special."

"Did you get anything else from the trunk? Tissue, bone fragments, anything like that?"

"Not a thing."

"So she wasn't killed in the trunk?"

"No, I don't think so. They might have stuffed her in there after they grabbed her, but that's all."

John hung up the phone a few minutes later. He knew little more now than he had a week ago, except for one small, but very important, detail.

He knew how soft Elizabeth's lips were.

Glancing at his watch, he stood up and made his way to the window, staring out across the common ground to Elizabeth's town house. It was almost time for her to be home. He waited every night and made sure her lights came on and then went off again. They'd spoken a few times since the kiss, but only about April and nothing more. He wondered if Elizabeth was becoming as aware of him as he was of her.

Just as he had the thought, she appeared suddenly on the sidewalk, carrying a small bag and walking slowly. John moved without thinking. He opened his door and called her name.

She looked up. There was a full summer moon shining between them and in the silver light, her dark hair shone like onyx. From a nearby open window, music—something classical—drifted in the air. It was a Mozart piece from *Don Giovanni,* John realized with a start. He couldn't believe he actually recognized it. All those operas he'd dozed through with Marsha must have soaked into his brain, after all.

Elizabeth's face stayed in the shadows, but she answered him over the haunting notes. "John! You're up?"

Leaving his front door open, he moved out onto his porch and motioned her over. "I was doing a little work," he lied, "and saw you going by. Hear anything interesting tonight?"

As she walked to him, he studied her face. Nothing could dim her beauty, but she looked tired. There were lavender shadows beneath her dark eyes, and lines on either side of her full lips. She looked tired and worried and almost at the end of her rope.

"I met the owner of the club. He's very strange, to say the least. His name's Lyndon Kersh. Ever heard of him?"

"I don't think so. But why don't you come in and tell me what he said?" John asked. "You look as though you could use a beer...or maybe a friend."

Their eyes locked in the darkness, and Elizabeth didn't have to speak for John to get his answer. Their kiss had scared her and she wanted to back off. Way off.

"Thank you," she said stiffly. "But I think it might be better if—"

"Daddy? Daddy, where are you?"

John turned instantly and stepped back to the open door. "I'm here, baby. On the front porch."

With a fist up to her eye and her latest Beanie Baby clutched to her chest, Lisa stumbled out to where he stood. "Is it morning? What are you doing outside?"

John bent down to her level. "I think the question is, what are *you* doing out of bed?"

She started to answer him, then looked over his shoulder and saw Elizabeth. "Who's that?"

John stood up. "This is Ms. Benoit, Lisa. Say hello."

He had to give credit where credit was due. Marsha believed in the rules of manners, if not for herself, for their daughter at least. Still half asleep, Lisa took two steps forward and held out her hand. "How do you do, Ms. Benoit. It's nice to meet you."

With a graceful swoop, Elizabeth bent down to Lisa's level and took her hand, completely charmed. "How do you do?" she repeated. "That's certainly a beautiful little bear you have there. I don't think I've ever seen a green teddy before."

"It's not a teddy," Lisa answered seriously. "It's a Beanie Baby. My mommy and I collect them. This one's not so 'special and Mommy lets me play with him."

"Really? May I see him?"

Standing to one side, John watched the interaction

in total amazement. He didn't know how he'd expected Elizabeth to relate to Lisa, but he found himself surprised by their easy communication.

The child handed her green bear over and Elizabeth exclaimed extravagantly, praising his color, his shape, his black-dot eyes. When she brought the stuffed animal to her face and rubbed it over her cheek proclaiming his softness, John felt himself twitch. At that moment he envied the toy.

Lisa smiled shyly. "Do you live here?" she asked.

"I sure do," Elizabeth answered. "Right over there." She pointed to her town house. "Maybe in the morning, you could come over and visit me. Would you like that?"

Lisa smiled, then all at once her expression changed. "I can't. I'm going on a picnic with my daddy." Then her forehead cleared. "But you could come with us! We're going to the zoo. You *could* come, couldn't you?"

Elizabeth glanced up at John, but before she could decline, he spoke up. "Why *don't* you?" he asked. "It'd be fun."

She rose slowly. "I...I don't want to intrude."

"You wouldn't."

She shook her head slowly. "I don't know...I was going to go over to April's apartment and talk to some of her neighbors again. I need to speak with

Linda Tremont and her brother again, too. I'm just about finished with their report for the S.E.C.''

Suddenly bored by the adult conversation, Lisa ran out to the grassy area in front of them and started dancing in the moonlight, holding her arms open wide and chasing lightning bugs. Giggling, she caught one, but let it go a moment later. In her tiny white nightgown, with her bare feet flashing in the moonlight, she looked like a fairy.

John spoke quietly. "You need a break, Elizabeth. And April wouldn't want you to make yourself sick over this. You look as if you're about to crash and burn."

"I know." She still held the bear, her fingers working into its fur. "I can't think of anything but April, though. The only time my brain rests is when I work or when I'm dancing." She kept her eyes on the stuffed animal. "And I don't like that. It...it's not good."

Without thinking, John reached out and ran a finger down her cheek. Beneath his touch, her skin was warm and satiny. When he lifted her chin, she stared at him with eyes as huge and dark as the night sky.

"Then come with us," he said. "One day isn't going to matter. April would say the same thing. You can tell me about Kersh then, too."

She started to answer, but Lisa ran up to them and held out her hand, demanding their attention.

"Look! I caught a lightning bug! Can I keep him, Daddy?"

Elizabeth dropped to her knees and smiled softly at Lisa. "Oh, you don't want to do that. His mommy and daddy would worry if he didn't come home. They'd wonder if he got lost and his brothers and sisters would all be sad."

John wondered if she had any idea of what she'd just said.

"Are you coming with us to the zoo?" Lisa asked.

Elizabeth glanced up at John, then back at his daughter. "No, I'm sorry. I can't go...but maybe another time."

The child's face fell. John moved closer to her and put his hands on her shoulders, meeting Elizabeth's eyes above her head.

"I think you need to get out of here," he said quietly.

Elizabeth hesitated, clearly torn, then she glanced down at Lisa again. The little girl's face was crestfallen. "You'd have a real good time," she said.

Elizabeth blinked. "Well...all right. I...I guess I'll tag along then."

John smiled his approval of Elizabeth's answer, then putting his hand on his daughter's head, he spoke in a mock-stern voice to her. "So now will you go back to bed?"

"Okay." She grinned and started back inside, but

before she reached the doorway, Elizabeth called to her.

"Lisa, wait. You forgot your bear." She held out the stuffed animal.

"That's okay," the child said after a moment. "You can sleep with him tonight, then in the morning you can bring him to the picnic." She stopped and made her face stern. "You can't take his tag off, though. They're ruined if you do that."

Elizabeth looked startled for a moment, then she smiled and hugged the bear. "I'll leave the tag right where it is," she promised. "And I'll take good care of him, I promise." She shot John a look he couldn't quite read, then turned and walked away, the light of the moon gleaming on her shoulders.

She disappeared into her town house a moment later, the bear still tucked close.

John turned and went inside, shaking his head.

That was one damned lucky bear....

ELIZABETH SET the stuffed toy on her nightstand, then picked up the photo she kept on the same table beside her clock. It was an old picture, one of her and April and their parents. Elizabeth studied the faces of her long-gone mother and father. For the first time in her life, she was almost grateful they were no longer here. Not knowing where April was would have been incomprehensible to their mother. April had always been her favorite and Elizabeth had understood completely. She hadn't minded; everyone loved April.

Somewhere along the line, Elizabeth had changed drastically, but when she was a child, her biggest ambition in life had been to be a mother herself. She'd babied every animal she could find, and every doll in the house was hers. Now she could see how far she'd carried on the role. She'd never seen herself as a mother, but April had been right. Elizabeth *had* told her what to do, how to live.

Elizabeth reached out and picked up the bear, Lisa Mallory's sweet expression forming in her mind. Would she ever have a child of her own? A child so smart and pretty and well-mannered? Elizabeth hadn't been around that many children, but it was obvious, even to her, how easily she'd clicked with the little girl. There was something about her, Elizabeth realized, that almost reminded her of herself. What was it?

She shook her head, then climbed into her bed, the cool clean sheets a soothing balm to her almost feverish mind and thoughts. She'd stopped by John's with the sole intention of telling him about Lyndon Kersh, nothing more. She'd walked away promising to spend a day at the zoo with him and his daughter. She tucked the bear in the crook of her arm and closed her eyes.

CHAPTER TEN

WHEN ELIZABETH heard the knocking on her door early on Sunday morning, she briefly considered ignoring it. It wasn't that she didn't want to go with John and Lisa—in fact, just the opposite. She wanted to go too much. She wanted to pretend, if only for a little while, that her life was normal. That April was in her apartment sleeping and this whole thing was some kind of nightmare. That wasn't the case, of course, so Elizabeth went to the door and opened it. When she saw Lisa Mallory's five-year-old excited face staring up at her, Elizabeth realized her reluctance went even deeper than she'd thought.

She could see herself with John, having a real relationship, having a life together, and the idea scared her half to death. She'd never planned on doing that.

Ignorant of Elizabeth's turmoil, Lisa grinned up at her. "You ready?" She hopped from one foot to the other, too excited to stand still. "Daddy says it's time to go. We got to leave early so we can see all the animals before it gets too hot!"

"Let me get my bag and your bear," Elizabeth answered, "then we can leave."

Seconds later they were walking down the dappled sidewalk under spots of bright summer sun, holding hands and chattering like old friends, Lisa clutching her stuffed animal once more. Walking beside the child, the small fingers intertwined with her hand, Elizabeth realized it felt so right. How weird! On the street John waited for them, leaning against the side of his pickup truck.

Elizabeth tried not to stare as they neared him, but finally she just gave up and let herself look. He had on his usual snug jeans and polished boots, but instead of a white starched shirt, this morning he wore a black T-shirt. His arms were crossed over his chest, and the sleeves had stretched to accommodate his biceps. A pale straw cowboy hat was perched on his head, and beneath the brim, his brown eyes were watching her watching him.

A blush heated her cheeks, but she pretended it was the sun and waved her hand like a fan in front of her face as if she were already hot.

"Good mornin'," he said, putting a finger to his hat when she reached him. "You look mighty nice for a picnic."

"Thanks."

Elizabeth glanced down at her sundress. She'd only tried on five before finally deciding. Sleeveless and loose, the straw-colored linen shift with its row of bone buttons down the front had seemed to be the coolest choice. John's appreciation for her choice was reflected in his eyes.

"Let's go! Let's go!" Lisa's exuberance saved Elizabeth from having to say more. They piled into the truck, the squirming child giving Elizabeth some much-needed distance between herself and John.

The zoo was already filling up by the time they went through the turnstiles, but there was plenty of room for everyone. For the next half hour, they toured the parklike setting, Lisa dashing ten feet for their every five. They saw the monkeys, the seals, the birds and the tiger, every step accompanied by Lisa's squeals of delight. Elizabeth refused to go into the snake house, though. She waited outside under a spreading live oak tree, and when John and Lisa emerged a few minutes later, the three of them walked out of the zoo to the park next door, John stopping by his truck to pick up his cooler.

Before they could pick a spot to eat, Lisa spied the swings and with an apologetic look at Elizabeth, John followed the child to the play area. In the shade of a nearby pecan, Elizabeth shook out the blanket, then opened the cooler, spreading out the deli fried chicken and deviled eggs he'd obviously bought the night before. Half a chocolate cake rested at the bottom of the chest, the frosting so thick and gooey Elizabeth couldn't resist poking her finger in it for a taste. Just as she was licking it off,

John appeared at her side, Lisa shrieking and calling out a few yards back as she tumbled down the slide she'd discovered.

John looked at Elizabeth, a frown marring his forehead. ''I could arrest you for that,'' he warned. ''Licking out of turn. It's a federal offense.''

Elizabeth grinned, then playfully stuck her finger back in the cake and pulled out an even bigger chunk of chocolate. Being with John and Lisa had brought out a side of her she hadn't felt in years— a fun side. She arched one eyebrow, then keeping her eyes on his, she deliberately brought her finger up to her mouth again. He reached out just as she parted her lips and grabbed her hand.

Then he brought it to his mouth. And slowly licked the chocolate off.

It was a corny move and Elizabeth giggled. A second later John laughed with her, a silly grin on his face. In that moment, though, that tiny fraction of time, she felt a warm long curl of the same something she'd felt when he'd kissed her the other night. She hoped it would mean less if she simply acknowledged it.

Desire. Plain and simple.

He felt it, too, but unlike her, couldn't pretend he didn't. His eyes darkened, and a kind of sizzling tension emanated from his body. He took a napkin from the bag he'd brought and wiped her fingers clean. When he finished, he looked at her with an expression so serious her heart skipped a beat.

"I'm glad you came with us today," he said simply.

"I am, too."

He still held her hand and had made no move to release it. His fingers were warm and his grip was hard. She had the sudden impression that everything he did would be this way—intense and focused. He might like to tease, but underneath the devastating grin there was more. A lot more. He glanced in Lisa's direction, then squeezed Elizabeth's hand again and spoke in a soft and nonthreatening way, changing the subject almost as if he understood how much she needed the extra room. "I talked to the tech about your car last night."

He explained everything, her hand still sandwiched between both of his. The gesture was comforting in a way she would have never expected.

"This doesn't mean anything concrete, Elizabeth. We still have no proof April's dead. And there's been nothing to show that the burglary of her apartment was anything but just that—a break-in."

She nodded, her throat too tight to say anything.

"Tell me about Kersh."

Elizabeth swallowed and then freed her hands to fuss with a loose piece of thread on the blanket. "He's strange, really strange. Dresses all in black, pale hair, pale eyes. He just appeared in the hallway between the stage and the dressing room. It was scary.''

"What'd he say?''

"He asked if any of the women were talking about April and then he said..." She stopped and took a deep breath, a ripple of anxiety running through her as she remembered. "He said I reminded him of an act he'd seen in Dallas. Of twins. H-he knew that April was a twin.''

"Do you think he knows?''

She shrugged helplessly. "I couldn't tell. He asked specifically if Tracy had said anything to me about April. I thought that was kinda weird, too.''

John went very still, his gaze directed once more to Lisa. For a moment he said nothing, then, "Tracy knows something,'' he said unexpectedly. "She came to me the first time I was there, and she's said things to you, too. She blew me off when I questioned her, but something tells me I should have stuck with her." He nodded slowly. "I'm bringing her in. I think she knows more than she's telling.''

"What do you think it is?''

"I don't know,'' he said slowly, "but if she didn't want to talk about it at the club and now this Kersh character is asking about her..." He grimaced. "There's a lot of money floating around in those places. Maybe April got involved in something she shouldn't have. Hell, you know the drill.

There's drug-selling, porn, you name it and you can buy it there.''

"Maybe so, but April didn't participate."

"Are you sure?"

"She never talked about it, and I haven't seen it if there is now."

"You're the new kid on the block. They aren't going to do their usual thing till they know they can trust you."

"That's not true," she said bluntly. "If anything illegal was happening, it'd be happening regardless. I'd know."

Lisa called out for them to watch her and they obliged, smiling and waving as she slid down a three-foot slide and shouted with glee. His eyes still on his daughter, John said, "Okay, then, let's suppose it's something else. Maybe it's Lansing himself? Hell, maybe it's Lansing *and* Tracy *and* Kersh." He glanced at Elizabeth, then focused once more on Lisa. "Maybe they have some under-the-counter deal going on."

"Not Tracy," Elizabeth answered. "She wouldn't be part of it."

"Why?"

"I...I don't know how to explain it, but beneath the bluster, she's..."

"Afraid?"

"Do you think?"

He shrugged again. "She did strike me as not

what she seemed, I'll give you that." His voice turned unexpectedly hard and brittle. "I thought it was probably a boyfriend problem."

Elizabeth kept her gaze on his face. His expression matched his voice, cold and unforgiving. It wasn't the first time she'd caught something in his manner, something that hinted at a past. She screwed up her courage to ask. "You…seem to understand that sort of thing," she said tentatively. "That first night you told me eighty percent of all murders are done by boyfriends or husbands. That's not just a statistic to you, is it?"

He kept his face turned away and concentrated on Lisa, but Elizabeth didn't need to see his expression to know what he was feeling. It was obvious in the way he tensed, the way his fingers tightened, the sense she got that there was a pain so great within him he couldn't contain it. She felt her heart turn over.

"No. It's not just a number to me." He paused, the bright sunlight and the cheerful little girl playing on the swings nearby making his next words more horrible than they already were. "My sister was killed by her husband."

"Oh, God…" Elizabeth brought her hand to her throat, then reached out automatically to John, putting her hand on his arm and squeezing the rock-hard muscles. "I'm so sorry, John."

"Me, too." Glancing across the way to where

Lisa was now hanging upside down on a swing, he covered Elizabeth's hand with his own. "Beverly was six years older than me, and I was a typical younger brother when we were growing up. We hardly ever spoke civilly to each other until we were in our late twenties. By then I was already on the force and she'd been married to her husband, Reed, for several years. He was an engineer. I never liked him, but when I tried to talk to her about him, she always blew me off."

"What happened?"

"He was a mean son of a bitch, that's what happened. He started hitting her when they'd been married only a few months, but no one told me. Beverly thought he was a good man and she could straighten him out if she just tried hard enough."

A gust of wind shook the crape myrtles behind them, and a shower of purple blossoms blew over the grassy expanse to their blanket. Like lavender snow, the tiny flowers piled up against the edge of the cooler. John reached out and picked up one of the blooms. His voice was bitter. "What a crock."

"Did they have any children?"

Lisa yelled again for him to watch and John did so, smiling, his words at odds with his expression. "No, thank God. They hadn't had kids."

"How long has it been?"

"She died three years ago," he answered. "On St. Patrick's Day. Reed had to work, and she'd gone out with some friends from work to celebrate. She was a librarian at a private school. When he came home early and she wasn't there, he waited up for her. He was sitting on the front porch when she drove into the drive at midnight. He met her on the sidewalk."

"They caught him, obviously."

His eyes were dark and flat when they met hers. "Yeah, they caught him. I almost wish they hadn't, though. I would have liked to deal with him myself."

"Oh, John…" The look on his face frightened her, but she understood completely. "It must have devastated your parents."

He nodded grimly. "It did. They haven't been the same since. They blame themselves, so on top of the grief, there's guilt, as well. When I divorced, it didn't help matters, either." He looked at Elizabeth. "My mom asked me once where she went wrong. How come her kids couldn't have 'normal' relationships. I didn't know what to tell her."

"Maybe they just didn't find the right people to have them with."

"I'd like to think that," John answered slowly. "Someday I want to try again. I want a family, a wife, more kids." He turned suddenly and looked at her. "How about you? You've just never found the right guy?"

Self-conscious suddenly, Elizabeth took her hand

from his arm. Had he somehow guessed her earlier thoughts? She didn't answer him right away, but instead, found herself thinking how they must look to a passing stranger. A nice family, she was sure. A beautiful child, a handsome father, a wife cool and proper in her linen sheath.... If they only knew.

"Elizabeth?"

"I never really thought about it," she lied. "Getting out of the business was all I could think about for years, then after I got my degree and started to work, all I could concentrate on was my job and trying to get April out as well." That, at least, was the truth. She really hadn't thought she'd ever be married or have a family. She wasn't that kind of woman and it wasn't the image she had of herself.

"You really hate dancing?"

She looked at him in surprise. "Oh, no—I love dancing. It makes me feel wonderful, free almost. Nothing matters but the music and the beat. If I'd been able to continue training after my father died, I'd probably be doing it professionally right now."

"But not the way April is."

"No." She shook her head. "I definitely wanted something different—for myself and for April."

"You could still dance professionally, couldn't you?"

"Gosh, no. Ballerinas are young, limber... I'm past that point."

His eyes softened with sympathy, then he nodded,

and a few seconds later, Lisa flitted back to where they were seated. For the remainder of the afternoon, Elizabeth let herself pretend they were what they seemed.

LISA FELL ASLEEP on the way home. John pulled up outside the complex, then gathered his daughter into his arms and climbed out of the pickup. He glanced over her head to where Elizabeth stood in the dusky shadows beside the truck. "Let me take her inside," he said. "Then I'll walk you home."

"That's not necessary—"

"I know," he interrupted. "But I want to, so humor me, okay?"

She smiled. "Okay. I'll wait on your porch."

He carried Lisa inside and set her down on the couch. He'd let her nap for a bit, then take her back to Marsha—she'd insisted Lisa come home tonight. Leaving his front door open, he went out to his darkened porch. The night air was humid and warm and filled with the sounds of crickets. A few scattered clouds drifted overhead, blocking the moonlight.

"She was bushed, wasn't she?" Elizabeth said.

John nodded. "It's hard work having that much fun. But I enjoy taking her out to do things like that. Her mom's idea of a good time is hitting the Galleria stores for a few hours. No sunshine factor there."

"You're a good father."

The words were softly spoken, but held plenty of conviction. John knew she was comparing him to her own father.

More touched than he would have expected, John said gruffly, "I could be a better one."

"I don't see how." She smiled. "You obviously love Lisa and want to do everything you can for her. What else does she need?"

The heat of the day had tugged at her hair, pulling down dark tendrils to hang about her face. What little makeup she'd worn to begin with was completely gone, and the only blush she had now was from the sun, arching across her nose and tinting both cheeks. In the square of light spilling from the open doorway, she looked like a different woman from the one he'd watched walk down the sidewalk in her prim and proper suit just a few weeks ago. One thing hadn't changed, though. She still took his breath away.

He stepped closer and raised a hand to her face. "Do you have any idea how beautiful you are?"

"I'm a mess," she protested.

"No," he said. "You're gorgeous."

She shook her head and started to say something else, but John didn't give her the chance. He brought his other hand up, cradled her face between his palms and began to kiss her. She tensed for just a moment, then gave in to the embrace.

Her lips were as warm and full as they had been the last time he'd kissed her, but this time there was an even stronger layer of tension hovering beneath the surface. Sliding his hands around her, he cupped her neck just beneath her hair line and pulled her into the shadows of the porch.

She moved closer to him, her breasts pushing against his chest, her hands on his shoulders, gripping them with surprising strength. He'd been thinking about kissing her all day long. From the minute she'd walked outside looking so cool and composed, he'd wanted to do this. To pull her to him, to feel her body against his own, to taste her mouth with his tongue....

The reality was even better than he'd imagined.

He hadn't thought of her perfume, which rose between them like heat from a scented candle. He hadn't thought of her dress, either, of the teasing barrier it would present between them—the feel of the linen against his hands, the warmth from the sun the fabric still held. And if he'd had a lifetime to think about the sweet curve of her buttocks beneath his hands, he could never have imagined how perfectly they fit into his palms.

He groaned and brought her closer, the sounds of her own desire low and needy in the night air.

Bringing his hand around, he slipped his fingers past the barrier of her top few buttons and cupped her lace-covered breast. John knew he was only torturing himself. This kiss was going nowhere with his daughter inside, but he could make the most of the moment he had, couldn't he? Elizabeth moaned into his mouth as his fingers found her nipple through her bra. He rubbed it gently as his lips left hers and trailed down the side of her neck. They swayed together on the porch, locked in their desire and trapped in their places, unable to move forward but unwilling to turn back.

From somewhere across the green, a door slammed, and Elizabeth jumped back, out of his arms. John looked up to see Mrs. Beetleman staring out from her porch. She met his stare with a "Hrmph," then stepped back inside her unit, closing the door behind her with as much force as she had a second earlier. It was just as well, he thought. If he took this as far as he could, Mrs. B's heart might not be able to take it.

He wasn't too sure his could, either.

Eyes huge and lips swollen, Elizabeth looked at him. It was too much—she was too beautiful, too sensual, too everything—and all he could think was to hell with Mrs. Beetleman. He started to pull Elizabeth back to him, but she put her hands on his chest and stopped him.

"This is crazy," she said, her voice breathless and husky.

"It doesn't feel crazy to me. In fact, it feels pretty

damn good." He tightened his arms, but again she stopped him.

"But it's scary..."

He narrowed his eyes. "Whether it scares you or not, you can't deny there's something between us, Elizabeth. You feel it, too, I know. I can tell."

"Just because I kissed you—"

"Hey," he interrupted, "I told you when we first met that I didn't have time for anything but the truth, and that hasn't changed."

Within his arms, she tensed, but only for a second. "What do you want me to say?" she whispered. "That I want you? That I wish you could walk across the lawn with me and come into my bedroom tonight? Is that what you want from me?"

"Would it be the truth?"

Her eyes locked on his, she nodded once.

"Then that's what I want to hear," he said.

"But it's not going to happen," she said.

He lifted his thumb and rubbed it over her bottom lip. "I can always hope that might change."

ELIZABETH CLOSED the front door behind her, then leaned against it, trembling. She felt like a teenager, crazy and confused and so aroused, she was almost dizzy. How had he done this to her? It had just been a kiss, dammit. What would happen to her if they actually made love? She'd heard of women who fainted when they had an orgasm. She'd laughed at the idea…but she wasn't laughing now.

Her legs gave out and she slid down the door to the floor with a thump. She raised her right hand to her lips. They felt hot and tender, and as the touch of her fingertip registered, she closed her eyes and imagined John's face just before his mouth descended on hers. He had long eyelashes—too long for a man—which had left dark shadows on his cheekbones… She groaned and dropped her fingers to her neck, where his whisker-roughened jaw stung her still. Her hands went even lower, and she cupped her breasts and pressed them together, her thumbs brushing her nipples, remembering the touch of his hand.…

April had told her once about a man she'd dated. She'd sworn he could turn her on just by looking at her. From across the room, she'd said, his eyes could heat her up and make her breath come fast and heavy. Without even touching her, he was able to bring her to the brink of orgasm.

Elizabeth brought her knees to her chest, then dropped her head to rest on them. She was making a mistake, a terrible mistake, and one way or another, she'd end up paying for it. What was she thinking?

She sat on the floor a little longer, then slowly she gathered herself together and started to stand. Just as she managed to get to her feet, a sudden knock on the door startled her and she gasped. When she looked out the window and saw John standing there, her knees threatened to go out again.

His expression was grim.

Panicking, she fumbled for the lock, throwing the door open a second later. "What's wrong?"

"I just got a call. It's Tracy Kensington. Somebody's beat the hell out of her."

Elizabeth's stomach lurched sickeningly. "Is she alive?"

"Barely. She's at Ben Taub Hospital, unconscious and hanging on, they don't know for how long. The responding officers found my card in her purse and called me."

"Do they know who did it?"

"No."

"Where was she?"

His jaw clenched. She could almost hear his teeth grinding. "In the parking lot…at the club."

Elizabeth reached behind her, seeking the door frame. She found it and held on.

"I'm on my way to the hospital now, but I wanted to let you know before I left. I'm dropping Lisa at Marsha's, then I'll go straight to Ben Taub from there. I'll call you."

"No. I'm coming with you."

"No way. You'll break your cover."

"You said she's unconscious. She won't even know I'm there." Elizabeth had already started toward the bedroom. "If she comes to, I'll make up a story," she said. "I'll tell her the police called me first since I work at the club. That makes perfect sense."

He started to argue, but then he looked in her eyes and read the stubbornness he knew was there. Without another word, he turned and she followed him, locking the door behind her.

CHAPTER ELEVEN

AS THEY ENTERED Ben Taub, Elizabeth was assailed by hospital smells, a mixture of antiseptics, cleaning fluids and anxiety. She hated it! When they were kids, April had had an emergency tonsillectomy, and Elizabeth had been convinced her twin was never coming home again. The bad association was only reinforced by April's appendectomy when they'd been on their own. That trip to the hospital had led to Elizabeth's dancing. To top it off was the institution in which they'd placed their mother. It, too, had the sharp scents that Elizabeth associated with fear.

She put aside her irrationality, ignored the worried faces of families sitting in the waiting room as she and John grabbed the nearest elevator. Tracy's room was easy to find. A black police officer was sitting just outside the door, his arms crossed and his eyes studying everyone who entered the corridor. Hefty and intimidating, his presence alone was enough to stop anyone, Elizabeth thought.

He stood, his face lighting up in recognition,

when he saw them rushing down the hall. "Big
John! Hey, man, how's it going?"

"Leonard! Good to see you. It's been a while,
huh?" John nodded to the door. "She's one of my
snitches," he explained. "How's it look?"

The man shook his head. "Bad, man, real bad. I
don't know if she'll hang on...."

Elizabeth's heart jumped. She put her hand on the
door and started to push it open, but with a deceiv-
ing quickness, Leonard reached out with one huge
hand and stopped her.

"Sorry, ma'am. Police officers only—unless
you're related."

John spoke quickly. "It's okay, Leonard. She's,
um, her sister."

The officer's gaze swung from Elizabeth's face
to John's. "Her sister?"

"That's right," Elizabeth replied, "her sister."

He hesitated a moment longer, then dropped his
hand and said to John, "I take it you're going to
stay in there while the 'sisters' visit?"

John nodded. "Of course."

At Leonard's nod, Elizabeth and John went inside
and crossed quickly to the bed. Elizabeth gasped
and suddenly wished the big cop outside *had* insisted she observe the rules. The figure under the
sheets, breathing with obvious difficulty, bore little
resemblance to the stunning redhead she knew as
Tracy. The right side of her face was so swollen her

features had almost disappeared, and what was left of her skin was bloody under the dressings. Her right eyebrow looked as if it had been singed off. One arm and one leg were encased in casts, and her neck was in a brace. For a moment Elizabeth wondered if a mistake had been made, but when she forced herself to look closer, beyond the tubes and bandages and dreadful injuries, she knew it was indeed Tracy in the bed.

"Oh my God..." Trembling, Elizabeth reached out and took John's arm. "I can't believe this."

John said nothing. All he did was stare at Tracy's once-beautiful face. Elizabeth glanced at him, but had to look away. Behind his professional expression, she'd glimpsed the raw horror in his eyes. She couldn't bear to see it. She knew he was staring at Tracy, but seeing his sister.

"What kind of monster would do something like this?" Elizabeth whispered. The machine nearest the bed began to hum, then beep. *Dear God,* she thought selfishly, *don't let this be April's fate. Please. I couldn't bear it.*

The door behind them whisked open and a woman bustled into the room, her white coat and attitude identifying her as a physician even before she spoke.

John and Elizabeth greeted her, John introducing them both and explaining their presence. He tilted his head to the bed. "What're her chances here, Doc?"

The woman stepped to the chrome side railing and put a hand on Tracy's arm. "I don't know," she answered truthfully. "The body can do a remarkable job repairing itself, but in this case someone's given it a tough task. She has internal injuries, as well."

John asked more questions and the physician answered them, but Elizabeth tuned it all out. Instead, she mimicked the doctor's touch, placing her own fingers on Tracy's other arm. Her skin was clammy. Elizabeth thought of Tracy's red cowboy boots and couldn't help the tears that welled in her eyes.

"I'm so sorry about your sister. I know this must be rough."

Elizabeth was confused by the doctor's words, then realized, of course, the cop outside must have spoken to her.

"I'm not her sister," Elizabeth confessed. "I'm just a friend. I don't think she has any family. Not here in Houston, anyway."

"Well, you should probably try and track them down, if you can." The physician's gaze went back to Tracy's face. Her voice was matter-of-fact. "They might be needed for arrangements."

IT SEEMED IMPOSSIBLE that their idyllic picnic had ended only hours before. As John pulled his pickup into the parking lot of the complex, Elizabeth lay her head back against the headrest and moaned. "I just can't believe it," she said, Tracy's ruined face and body floating through her mind.

John shut off the truck's engine and they sat in the darkness. When they'd left Tracy's room a female detective had been outside, leaning against the wall and visiting with Leonard. John had stopped and talked to her, introducing her to Elizabeth as Lieutenant Stacinski.

"Stace said a passerby found her in the parking lot and called for an ambulance. The club's closed on Sundays, so I assume Tracy must have stopped by for some reason."

"How long had she been lying there?"

"No one knows."

"No witnesses?"

"No." He shook his head. "I'm not officially on the case—yet—but I told Stace everything that's been going on and suggested she bring in Lansing and sweat him. I gave her Kersh's name, too."

They stepped from the truck and crossed the grass to the sidewalk leading to Elizabeth's home. Walking silently, each lost in their own thoughts, they made their way to her front door.

Elizabeth had to ask the question she'd been thinking since the moment she'd seen Tracy's ravaged face. "Do you think whoever hurt Tracy...has done the same thing to April?"

"I don't know, Elizabeth," John answered slowly. "I certainly hope not."

She started to cry. "I...I can't stand it. It's so...so inhuman."

He pulled her into his arms. "I know, I know." His voice was a deep rumble at her ear. "When we find the son of a bitch, it's gonna be real hard not to do the same thing to him that he did to her."

Elizabeth hiccuped against his chest. "I thought you said you believed in letting the judges decide the punishment."

"I do," he answered, "but that doesn't mean I don't *want* to dish out a little punishment of my own sometimes, too."

They stood quietly, locked together in their shared anger and grief, then Elizabeth finally pulled back. "Will you be there when they bring in Greg?"

"Absolutely."

"Are you going to ask him about April?"

"One way or the other, I'm going to ask him about everything," he promised. "And he'll answer, too, don't you worry."

She nodded once, then stepped out of his arms and unlocked her door. For a moment she thought of asking him in. She *wanted* to bring him inside—and into her bed. Into her heart. But she couldn't, not tonight. Not with the haunting image of Tracy's ravaged face in her mind and all the confusion it had brought to the forefront. Elizabeth lifted her eyes to John's. Their gazes connected, and she knew she didn't have to explain. He understood completely.

He leaned down and kissed her long enough and hard enough to almost change her mind, but then he turned and left. She closed the door behind him and switched on the light…

…and screamed.

JOHN WAS HALFWAY across the grassy expanse between his town house and Elizabeth's when he heard the scream. His heart leapt into his throat and he pivoted, his hand on his .44. He jerked the weapon out of the holster even before his feet began to run. Two seconds later he was at Elizabeth's porch where he didn't even try for subtlety. He lifted his boot and kicked in the door.

Elizabeth spun around and opened her mouth to scream again, but as soon as she saw it was him, her terrified expression changed and his name came out in a sob. His brain registered the scene in the space of a second.

Someone had vandalized her home.

From the soft ivory couch to the books in the bookcase, everything in the room had been slashed, ripped or torn apart. Paintings were off the walls and lying in shattered pieces of glass and frame. Cushions from the chairs were tossed on the floor with their stuffing in piles around them. The delicate wooden end tables were upside down, their legs snapped off and apparently used to smash what couldn't be moved—such as the glass-fronted curio cabinet, which now held nothing but shattered empty shelves, the crystal and silver it had been protecting strewn from one end of the room to the other.

"Come over here," he commanded. "Watch where you step."

She picked her way toward him, her face white, her eyes enormous. When she got to his side, he reached into his pocket with one hand and retrieved his keys. "Go to my place," he said, "call 911, and wait there."

She started to say something and he shook his head. "Now, Elizabeth. Just do it."

She stepped past him to the porch, and he turned to watch her as she hurried to his house and disappeared inside. With Elizabeth safe, he was able to focus, and he advanced into the house, clutching his gun. Glass and God only knew what else crunched beneath his boots with each step. He lowered the gun but kept it out before him, his eyes darting from one side to the other in a continual sweep. The floor plan was the same as his place, so he knew it well, knew the nooks where someone could hide, knew the places where someone could pop out and surprise him with their own weapon pointed at his chest.

But no one did. The town house was empty. Before he even got all the way down the hall, he knew they were gone. He had a sixth sense about these kinds of things, but he always followed up with careful checking, too. He kept the weapon before him until he reached the rear of the house, then he lowered it slowly to his side and surveyed what had been Elizabeth's bedroom.

The mattress had been lifted off the box spring and slashed open from one end to the other. Springs and foam padding littered the carpet along with what had been the pillows. The linens had been torn as well as the draperies; the chest and every drawer from the dresser and nightstand had been emptied, the items scattered. On the wall above the bed, a pale rectangle told him where a painting had hung—the painting that was now twisted out of its frame and slashed as violently as the bed.

"Mallory! Where are you?"

At the sound of the booming voice, John automatically lifted his gun, then dropped it just as fast when he recognized the caller. "Back here, Stan! In the bedroom." He heard the officer give the all clear to his partner, then a few seconds later, the uniformed cop appeared at the door. Stan Vasquez had been on the force as long as John. They'd been rookies in the same class at the academy.

"Fast response, Stan."

"Believe it or not, we were right around the corner when we caught the call. Doing a follow-up on a burglary." For the first time the tall Hispanic cop glanced around. "God almighty," he exclaimed. "Somebody had a party, huh?"

John nodded grimly and said nothing, finally slipping his weapon back into the holster beneath his arm.

Vasquez walked into the room, his sturdy black brogans plowing through the mess. He looked around him and shook his head. "I don't think I want to know how you're involved in this one, Mallory. There's one helluva good-looking broad outside, though, asking for you. How do you do it? How does an ugly SOB like you manage to hook these good-lookin' babes?"

John grinned and brushed past his old friend. "It's my sterling personality, Stan. What can I say?"

"Sure, right…"

When John returned to the living room a second later and took in Elizabeth's face, his humor completely disappeared. He walked up to her. "I thought I told you to wait at my place."

"I couldn't." She took a deep shuddering breath. "When I saw the other officers get here, I figured it was safe. They're gone, aren't they?"

He knew what she meant. "Yeah. Whoever did

it, did it fast and took off. There had to be more than one, too, I'd say.'' He glanced at his watch. It was past midnight. "We weren't at the hospital more than a couple of hours.''

She stepped into the mess, her features forming a mask of disbelief. "Who would do this? It...it's incredible.''

"Someone who was mighty mad, I'd say. This kind of destruction isn't normal or even aimless. It's real damned personal.''

She picked up a pillow and was trying futilely to put some of the stuffing back into it. He stilled her movements with a hand to her wrist. "Go check whatever you had that was valuable. Your jewelry, a camera...stereo, whatever.''

She nodded and walked off in numb silence. In ten minutes she was back. "I think my pearls are gone. The television and stereo are there...but they've been destroyed.''

"What about cash?''

"I never keep much here. It'd just disappear—'' She broke off abruptly and turned away from him, but not before he knew what she was about to say.

...*because April would help herself to it.*

Moving to her, John slipped his arm around her shoulder and squeezed. "Who could be this mad at you, Elizabeth? Think hard. This was no random act.''

Her eyes filled with tears and she shook her head.
"I...I don't know."

"Someone at the club?"

"They don't know where I live." She dropped
the pillow to the floor. "They don't even know who
I really am."

"Maybe. Maybe not."

She walked farther into the room. She stood still
amid the mess, then slowly turned in a circle. "Have
you ever seen anything like this before? This...total
trashing?"

"Yeah." He walked to the hearth and picked up
the photo of her and April. It'd taken a beating, too;
the frame was twisted, the glass broken out. The
photo had been ripped into two neat pieces. He set
them back on the mantel. "I had a case once where
a guy was blowing the whistle on his employer. He
worked down on the Ship Channel for a chemical
plant, and they were dumping stuff you wouldn't
believe into the channel every night. He'd taped a
meeting that showed the bigwigs knew what was
going on. They sent some thugs over to find the tape
and teach the guy a lesson."

"I can almost understand that, but this?" She
looked around, then her hand went to her throat.
"Do you think this could be the same guy who
broke into April's? Maybe he was looking for something? And when he didn't find it, he decided to
come here?"

"It's possible. Did she ever give you things to keep?"

"No, but that doesn't mean anything. She could have left something here and not told me. She stayed in the spare bedroom, and I never go in there."

"Well, it's a little late, but why don't you go in there now and look around? See if there's anything you don't recognize."

She nodded, then started back down the hallway just as Stan Vasquez came into the living room. She stopped when he appeared.

"I've checked the doors and all the windows." He turned to speak to Elizabeth. "Could you have possibly left the place unlocked, ma'am? There's no sign of forced entry anywhere. My partner's canvassing the neighbors, but so far, nobody's heard a thing. Apparently he walked right in."

"No..." John and Elizabeth spoke at the same time. She nodded to him to go ahead.

"We left together about two hours ago," John said. "I heard her lock the door."

"And I unlocked it when I came in," she added, her expression puzzled. "That's crazy. Are you sure...?"

"I checked. No one broke in to do all this, I can promise you that."

She shook her head. "I...I just don't understand."

Stan asked, "Is there an ex-husband? An old boy-friend?"

"No, neither."

As Elizabeth answered Stan, John's mind turned over the possibilities slowly and carefully, then suddenly, with blinding clarity, a possibility shot into his brain. He hated the idea and he wanted to dismiss it as quickly as it'd arrived. But he couldn't. It was too obvious and he couldn't believe he hadn't thought of it sooner. He cautioned himself to slow down and think it out. Talking to Elizabeth might dredge up another name, another suspect. He'd have to ease his way into it. He could be wrong.

But if he wasn't, Elizabeth would be crushed.

ELIZABETH KNEW it was probably not a good idea, but hours later, after everyone had left and they'd discussed who might have a key to her place, John offered her the use of his spare bedroom, and she was too wiped out to do anything but accept. Deep down, she acknowledged that chances were pretty good she might not end up sleeping in the same bed Lisa did when she slept over.

But that idea didn't bother Elizabeth as it would have a few weeks ago. In fact, it sounded pretty damned good right now. She wanted—no, *needed*—a man's arms around her. For the first time in longer than she could remember, Elizabeth wanted comforting, help, wanted to simply turn all her problems over to someone else and let *them* worry—for a change.

Standing in John's guest bathroom, she shook her head and finished brushing her hair with the spare Cinderella hairbrush she'd found in one of the bathroom drawers. She'd just bathed with Minnie Mouse bubble bath and washed her hair with Donald Duck shampoo. Self-conscious but too tired to really care, she stepped out into John's hall wearing only the oversize T-shirt he'd given her. She could have dug through the mess at her place for something, she supposed, but it had seemed an overwhelming task when she'd walked into her bedroom and seen the destruction. She didn't relish the thought of putting on something a stranger had touched, either.

John was waiting for her in his living room. The only light in the room was coming from the kitchen, but she didn't need more illumination to see. His eyes swept over her and left a trail of sparks that pricked her skin.

She came farther into the room and picked up the drink he'd poured her. She took a sip and then another. The liquor burned her throat, but the stinging sensation quickly changed to a steadying warmth. She sat down beside John and, still holding the drink, let her head fall back against the sofa cushion.

So gradually she hardly noticed, a calm slipped over her. John seemed to sense she didn't want to talk about the destruction, and if he'd spoken or tried to tell her to relax, she wouldn't have been able to do either; but between his steady silence and the strong drink, she found a measure of peace. He would take care of her, she thought, cradling her glass. This man could take care of her.

She emptied the tumbler, then set it down and turned her head to face him. His expression was shadowed from the light behind them, but a single ray fell on his right temple. She reached up and traced the tiny moon-shaped scar beside his eyebrow.

"My sister's revenge," he said quietly. "She got fed up with me one day and let me have it with a teacup."

It was totally out of character for her, but without understanding why and not trying to think any more about it, Elizabeth leaned over and pressed her mouth against the thin curved line. His skin was soft beneath her lips, and he smelled good, clean and soapy. He shifted to face her directly.

His eyes were black pools. Without breaking the look between them, he lifted her chin with his fingers and leaned close. Their lips met, tentatively at first, then the kiss grew more heated until it suddenly ignited. Elizabeth found herself pressing even closer to him, wishing there was nothing between them, not even the flimsy barrier of the T-shirt she wore.

As always, he seemed to read her mind. His

hands slipped under the shirt to her naked skin. He spanned her rib cage with his fingers, then moved upward until he was brushing the underside of her breasts. She felt his thumbs and then the edge of his nail as he gently raked it across one sensitive nipple, then the other.

She moaned against his mouth, and her hands found the buttons on his shirt. He'd obviously bathed and changed while she had, and the newly laundered shirt crackled as she struggled with the buttons. A second later his chest was bare as she pushed the two sides of the shirt open and slid her hands inside.

She ran her fingers over his broad shoulders, then dipped her head to plant moist kisses on his chest. She felt his moan as much as heard it, and she tortured him a second longer. But then he rose up and lifted the T-shirt over her head, then pressed her, naked and needy, back against the cushions.

Hovering over her, his shirt open, her body trapped by his knees on either side, he stopped. His eyes took in every inch of her body, and just as before, his gaze seemed to have a tension of its own, touching her and moving her, bringing her even higher. He looked for so long that she raised her arms to pull him back to her, and with a deep rumbling groan, he gave in.

CHAPTER TWELVE

HE'D SEEN Elizabeth dance, her body barely covered, but John still wasn't ready for the perfection stretched out before him. For the first time, he felt as though he was really seeing Elizabeth, seeing the self she tried so hard to hide from him and everyone else. The bare emotion on her face made her all the more human in his eyes...and all the more appealing.

He covered her lips with his own, and his desire grew. He kept one hand at the curve of her neck, then dropped his fingers to his belt buckle.

"Let me," she whispered.

They shifted places on the couch and then she was poised above him, her hair hanging down around them and brushing his chest. Her nails were short and blunt, and they teased his skin as she released his buckle and then tugged at his pants.

Naked a moment later, John reached up and pulled her toward him, but instead of lying down, she shook her head and resisted. With her eyes on his, she moved over his body, dropping kisses on his throat, his shoulders, his chest. When he could stand it no more, he put his hands on her shoulders and dragged her to him. He rolled her over on the couch so that she lay stretched out. His hands made their way over her skin just as she'd touched him a moment before, but she didn't stop him as he had her, and his fingers glided over her, discovering every curve and dip. His mouth followed, and she arched her back to press into his kisses, murmuring his name with growing urgency.

He wanted to make the moment last, to kiss her and touch her and have her plead for him when it was time, but in the end, he was the one who begged. There were no words spoken, though, no whispered entreaty, no appeals for mercy. He asked with his body, and she answered with hers.

THEY'D MOVED to the bed for a second bout of love-making, and now, afterward, she lay there on her side, one of his arms wrapped around her body. She felt she understood John Mallory a lot better than she had before.

Understood him and…loved him?

The thought startled her and she moved to sit up, pulling the sheet with her to cover her breasts.

"Are you cold?" he asked, reaching out to trace a finger down her spine.

"N-no," she answered. "Just…thinking."

He folded his arms behind his head and watched

her. "Must not be good thoughts if they're making you shiver."

"None of my thoughts has been too great lately," she confessed. They moved easily into the conversation and Elizabeth realized how comfortable she felt. "Too much is happening."

"It seems that way, doesn't it? Life can get crazy."

"But you're a cop," she said. "I thought all you guys liked crazy."

"We deal with it at work. But when it's time to come home, that's a different story. I want a safe haven then. Dinner cooking in the kitchen and my daughter at the door."

His answer echoed Tracy's dressing-room observation. *That kinda guy doesn't bother with women like us.... He'd want Donna Reed at home, you can bet on it.* Elizabeth tuned out the memory to focus on the moment. "You really miss her, don't you?"

"You could chop off my right arm and I'd need it less," he admitted. "When Marsha and I divorced, I sued for full custody, but it was a lost cause. The judge was a family friend of Marsha's father and said kids belonged with their mother. That was that. I was lucky to get her one night a week."

He rolled onto his side and pulled her down to face him. She couldn't read his expression, but she tensed, anyway, sensing something. After a moment he spoke.

"Elizabeth…about April…"

She waited.

"I know you love her." His gaze was intense. "In fact, you really care for her almost as a parent would, right?"

"Yes…"

"Then what I'm about to say will be extra hard for you to consider, but I want you to promise me you'll at least hear me out, okay?"

Her mouth went dry, but she nodded.

He spoke quickly, as if he had to get the words out before he changed his mind. "Have you ever considered that April might have planned all this? That she might be behind her disappearance?"

She stared at him, confused. "What are you saying?"

Instead of answering immediately, he eased himself to the edge of the bed and stood. With his back to her, it was easier, John thought. He didn't have to look into those dark puzzled eyes. But he couldn't do it that way, the coward's way. He picked up his pants, pulled them on and faced her. "I suggested this when we first started, but I've got to ask you again. What makes you so sure April didn't just leave?"

Her mouth fell open in surprise, then she snapped

it shut and answered him. "I'd say an abandoned car with bloodstains in it, for one thing."

He shook his head gently. "That's not proof, Elizabeth. It just means we found your car. Nothing more."

"How can you say that? April's blood was in it."

"It could have been planted."

Elizabeth started to say something else, then stopped. Pulling the sheet from the bed, she stood up, wrapped it around herself and stared at him. "Where are you going with this?" she said quietly. "I don't understand."

He walked around the edge of the bed and stopped directly in front of her. Placing his hands on her warm shoulders, he stared at her and cursed himself for what he was about to ask. Did she know what was coming? Did she suspect anything? He looked into the bottomless well of her eyes, but he couldn't find an answer.

"Someone broke into April's apartment. Someone beat up Tracy Kensington. Someone broke into your place. Do you think it's remotely possible April could be behind any of this, Elizabeth?"

She blinked once. Then again. "You mean... could she have planned it all?"

"That's exactly what I mean. It's entirely possible—"

She started shaking her head and held out a hand as if to stop his words. "Oh, no..."

"Wait! Hear me out. You said you and April had a fight the night before. She was angry at you, upset because you wanted her to stop dancing and because she felt you were trying to run her life." He tightened his grip. "Think about it, Elizabeth. If April was really angry, how would she strike out at you?" He answered when Elizabeth didn't. "She'd ruin your life. She'd turn it upside down and inside out, and what kind of confusion she didn't create, you'd create yourself because you'd be worried sick over her."

Elizabeth shook her head again, more violently this time. "No! She might have planned her disappearance, but that's all!"

"It's just a thought, but think about it. You went to her apartment and tried to clean it up. The guy in the mask could have been waiting for you to show up. You contacted the people at the club, too. April would know you'd do what you had to to get in with them, and she'd know who'd be the first one to talk to you—Tracy. But now Tracy can't talk. Why?"

With a cry, Elizabeth tore herself from his grip and stepped back. "This is nuts. April wouldn't do this. She wouldn't! There's no reason, for God's sake."

"People don't always have reasons we know about. Like I said, maybe she was just plain mad."

"She was angry, yes, but why not simply disappear? Why all the other stuff?"

"I don't know for sure," he said slowly. "But maybe she had other people upset with her. Maybe she *had* to disappear and make it look good. Then she would have had to arrange the break-in to make it all seem authentic."

Elizabeth shook her head, over and over, her dark hair swinging against her shoulders. "No. No way. Not my sister. She wouldn't do that."

"Just think about it. Consider it," he said quietly. "She might have planned her disappearance, and then things got out of hand. She must have had help—maybe whoever was in on it with her decided to take it in a different direction."

Silence filled the room, heavy and tense, then finally she lifted her gaze. He could see she was vacillating. He read it as clearly as he had read the shadows he'd seen there, the shadows he'd seen but hadn't understood until she'd revealed her family history.

He reached out and tucked a long strand of black silk behind her ear. "Just think about it," he said quietly. "It's a possibility I believe you need to consider."

IT TOOK ELIZABETH four days to get her place cleaned up. She called the club and said she had a personal problem and wouldn't be back. Greg had hardly seemed to care. When the last load of garbage was carted off, she stood in the middle of the living room and stared at the only plant left—an ivy she'd rescued and stuck back into its pot. She'd saved her couch and one armchair, but the bed had had to go, and there had been only a few knick-knacks here and there that she'd kept. The papers she'd been able to salvage from her study, business and personal, she'd simply thrown into a box to sort out later.

She walked into the almost bare space and sank to the floor. She had only one wish: that she could make her mind as empty as the room. Ever since Sunday her brain had been in utter turmoil. When she wasn't thinking of what kind of mistake she'd made by sleeping with John, she was thinking of what he'd suggested the night after they'd made love.

Could April have somehow faked her own disappearance?

Elizabeth shook her head in the barren silence of her home. It just didn't make sense. Why would April do such a thing? Sure, she owed Elizabeth money, but that had never bothered her before, certainly not enough to run away. And yes, they'd had a fight, but when *weren't* they fighting?

And what about the car? Even if April had planned her abrupt departure, would she do something so elaborate? Blood on the seats and abandoning the vehicle on Dowling? And what about that shoe? Elizabeth had wondered about it ever since the cop on the street had held it up for her to identify. She'd come home and checked immediately. The corresponding plastic box had sat on her closet shelf, empty. It made no sense at all because she knew she hadn't worn the shoes and left one in the trunk. Elizabeth didn't do things like that. And April would never have borrowed *them*. They were too staid. Too boring.

Nothing about this situation made any sense to her, but John was used to making sense out of stranger situations than this. He'd said enough to make her think twice about his theory—more than twice, actually. What if he was right? She let her brain play it out. What could have happened to April that was bad enough to make her run? Had she fallen in with the wrong crowd? Was someone after her? If they were, why? Why would she disappear?

Elizabeth closed her eyes and remembered their last fight. April *had* seemed different that night. Edgier, nervous, more defensive than usual. Something had been bothering her, but what? Elizabeth searched the nooks and crannies of her memory, but couldn't come up with a single clue. For the millionth time since all this had started, she longed for the mental connection she and her twin had once shared, so she could tap into it and know where April was. She'd actually tried once or twice, concentrating her mind like a laser on April, but... nothing.

As if it couldn't face that particular problem any longer, her brain switched gears and went to the other chief topic it'd been dwelling on—John. The night they'd spent together had been so wonderful, it had terrified Elizabeth. She'd packed the Cinderella hairbrush and the T-shirt and found herself an inexpensive motel. John had tried to conceal the frustration in his eyes, but he hadn't succeeded. She'd walked out to her rented car with his gaze on her back, her awkward excuse about not wanting to impose any longer still hanging in the tension-filled air.

It was a bald-faced lie and both of them had known it.

But John was too much of a gentleman to call her on it, and she was too much of a coward to tell him the truth. To tell him how much he scared her. To tell him how good it felt to have his arms around her. To explain why she couldn't let herself depend on him—or worse, love him.

And on top of everything, there was Tracy. Every day brought a different medical crisis for the dancer, and the doctors still weren't sure if she was going to make it. Each time Elizabeth visited, she would stare down at the bed and see her sister's pale face lying there, instead of Tracy's.

It was all too much. She couldn't take it anymore.

Elizabeth put her head down on her knees and began to cry.

JOHN NODDED to the officer sitting in front of Tracy's hospital room. Leonard was off today, but the other cop recognized him, as well he should. John had visited every day, sometimes twice a day. He knew if he could get a name from Tracy—just the name of the son of a bitch who had done this to her—he'd be one step closer to finding out what had happened to April Benoit.

Of course, Elizabeth didn't see the possibility of her sister having set this disaster into motion, and he hadn't really expected her to. He wasn't one hundred percent sure himself. There were only two things he was sure of: Elizabeth wanted nothing to do with him after their night together, and he couldn't wait to see her again.

She had made her feelings more than apparent by leaving Monday morning and checking into a motel. John had wanted to protest and try to convince her to stay, but he'd stopped himself. She was too independent and stubborn for that technique to work, and if he didn't recognize that by now, they'd never have a serious relationship.

And a serious relationship with Elizabeth was exactly what he wanted. Half-asleep, with his arms wrapped around her and the fragrance of her hair drifting up to him, John had realized that startling fact. She was much more than a gorgeous woman. She was a loving giving person who cared more about what happened to her sister than to herself.

And he had fallen in love with her without realizing it.

John pushed open the hospital door, the hydraulic hinge at the top whispering quietly. Tracy looked over with a fearful expression. It was the first time he'd seen her awake.

Some of the fear dissipated when she recognized him, but too much of it remained. What was she scared of most? he wondered. Telling him who'd hurt her...or not telling him?

He walked to the bed and stopped at the foot of it. "How you doing? You've been a real sleeping beauty. I've been here every day, and this is the first time you've been awake."

She nodded, then grimaced instantly at the movement. "Hurts..." she murmured.

"I'll bet it does."

She reached out, using the arm not in the sling, for the plastic cup on the swing-around table beside the bed, but she was a few inches short. Before she could try again, John moved around to that side of the bed, lifted the cup and held it to her mouth. Her eyes met his, then she slowly pulled the straw closer to her and sipped. The effort, small as it was, seemed to drain her. She let her head fall back to the pillow, her cheeks paler than they'd been a moment before. Her eyes shuttered down.

John put the cup back on the table. "Tracy," he said, "I know this is tough for you, but we need to talk. You've got to tell me who did this to you."

She stayed motionless for so long, with her eyes closed, he wondered if she'd drifted back to sleep.

"Tracy? Are you listening to me?"

After a moment, she opened her eyes, but she didn't speak.

"You've got to tell me who did this to you," he repeated. "But you'll be safe, I promise. There's a cop right outside your door and he's not leaving."

"A-and…later?" she croaked. "Wh-what about later?"

"We'll put the guy in jail. You won't have to worry about him later."

No response.

"We *will.*"

She stayed silent.

"Who was it?" He reached out and put his finger against her cheek. "Lansing?"

She didn't even blink.

"Was it Lyndon Kersh?" He looked down at her and tried to contain his growing frustration.

She moved her head slowly until she was facing the wall away from him. He'd been dismissed.

John walked around to the other side of the bed,

anyway. "Did this have anything to do with April?"

She said something then, something he didn't understand. He bent down.

"Go away." The words were tortured. "Please. Leave me alone."

John put his face on the same level as hers. The skin across her temple and down her cheeks was a startling combination of purple and black. Suddenly the injustice of it all hit him square on. A tight catch came into his chest. He tried to ignore it and what it meant, then stopped himself. He *ought* to be feeling it, he told himself. The emotion behind the painful sensation was anger, and this kind of anger was good. It fueled his determination.

"We brought in both of them," he pushed. "But Kersh's attorney wouldn't let him say squat. And Lansing told us he was with someone the night this happened to you, one of the girls he called Brownie. She backed up his alibi when I called her. You know her?"

The green eyes flared.

"She said he was with her all night." He let the words linger, then repeated them for emphasis. "*All* night."

"Son of a bitch," she managed to get out.

John nodded. "Yeah, I'd agree with you there. Lansing strikes me as a son of a bitch, too. A *lying* son of a bitch."

She jerked her eyes nervously to the door but stayed silent.

"We can protect you," John whispered. "Just give me a name. Tell me who did this." He waited another beat, then spoke again. "It was Lansing, wasn't it?"

Her gaze went to the ceiling and stayed there for a moment, then it came back to John's face. Her eyes were filled with tears, liquid and shimmering, as much an admission as if she'd spoken. The emerald color was so bright and shattering, it looked almost unreal. Tracy nodded slowly.

In spite of the woman's pain, a ripple of something that felt like victory washed over John. Guilt came on its heels, but he didn't really give it time to register. "Why? Why'd he do it, Tracy?"

She closed her eyes. A single tear squeezed out of one eye and trickled down to the pillow. She stayed quiet and didn't move.

"You know what happened to April, don't you? You were going to tell me, but you got scared. And Lansing was afraid you'd eventually get up your courage and come back to me, so he did this to keep you quiet. Was he trying to kill you or just give you a warning?"

She spoke without opening her eyes, her exhausted voice weak but stubbornly insistent. "I...can't tell you anything...about April."

"You can't or you won't?"

He waited for an answer, but the only sound in the room came from the heart monitor beside the bed. Finally he realized she wasn't going to say any more. She'd been scared, and she was sure silence was the only way she'd live. John turned from the bed and started for the door, but at the last minute, just as he put his hand on the lever, she spoke.

"T-tell her...be careful..."

John froze, then pivoted and came back to the bed. "Who? Who needs to be careful?"

"Elizabeth." Tracy took a deep shuddering breath. "He...knows. Gr-Greg knows who she is."

John sat down beside the bed and Tracy began to talk.

"WE'VE PICKED UP Lansing again and we're bringing him in."

John's voice sounded grim over the telephone and Elizabeth's fingers tightened on the receiver. She'd come back to the motel after cleaning up the town house and had begun to work a bit, Linda Tremont's case still hanging over her head and demanding attention. She'd had to reconstruct a great deal of her notes, but she'd managed after calling Betty and then Linda to confirm a few final details. As soon as she'd put down the phone, it'd rung again. At John's voice, all thoughts of work fled her mind.

"Tracy told me this morning he's the one who beat her up."

Elizabeth's gasp filled the phone line. "My God, why? Why would he do something like that?"

"I don't know for sure, but I'm on my way downtown to find out. Officially. The case has been labeled an attempted homicide and I'm on it. Two uniforms are bringing him in."

Elizabeth's mouth went dry and it was hard to speak. "Did Tracy say anything about April?"

"Not really. I pressed her on it, but she wouldn't give me what I needed."

"I want to come up there."

"Absolutely not!" His voice was sharp, and he seemed to realize it, because he softened it when he spoke again. "I'm sorry, Elizabeth, but that's impossible. Let me handle it. I promise you, I'll call the minute I know anything."

"John, please…"

"Elizabeth, listen to me. There's something else going on, something more important than what Tracy told me. I've got two officers on their way to your motel now. They'll be there any minute. They're going to stay with you for a while."

"Why?"

"Greg Lansing knows who you are. He knows you're April's sister."

Bile filled her throat almost instantly, and Elizabeth sat down on the edge of the bed. "He knows? How can he know? It's impossible."

"Tracy figured it out. She said April had shown

her a photograph of you. Once Tracy realized what
was going on, she told Lansing.''

''He's behind everything,'' Elizabeth said. ''He
took April, John, I know he did. Then he broke into
her apartment and then my place—''

''We don't know any of that for sure yet. We'll
have to talk to him.''

A loud knock sounded on the door of her room.
''H.P.D.,'' a voice called out. ''Miss Benoit, you in
there?''

John spoke urgently into her ear. ''Don't just
open the door, Elizabeth. Tell him to hold up his
shield so you can read the number and his name-
plate. The guys I sent are Clark and Stanley.''

''Okay, just a minute.'' Her pulse pounding in
her ears, she made her way to the door and looked
out the peephole. ''Hold up your shield,'' she said.
''I want to read the number.''

The man fumbled for a minute, then held up a
shiny brass plate. She read off the name and number. ''S.P. Clark, No. 1034.''

She ran back to the phone and repeated the man's
name and number.

''That's him,'' John answered. ''Let them in, then
come back to the phone.''

She did as he instructed, and the two officers
stepped inside and took off their hats, their presence
intimidating in the small room. After introducing
themselves, one went immediately toward the bath-

room and looked inside, while the other opened the closet door and peered in. She picked up the phone again.

"They're here," she said shakily. "Now what?"

"Now what is you sit tight. Don't leave the room. Don't make any phone calls. Let the police answer the door if someone comes knocking. If Lansing's behind this, something tells me he might not have done it all on his own. We'll have him here, but who knows who else is out there running around."

"I understand." Her voice trembled, but she was grateful it wasn't as shaky as she actually felt.

"It'll be okay, Elizabeth. I promise. We're going to get this bastard and he will not hurt you. I won't let that happen, count on it."

He spoke with such confidence she allowed herself to relax a fraction. "Why would Greg do all this? I don't understand it."

"I don't know the answer to that question right now, but by the end of the day, I will."

CHAPTER THIRTEEN

HOUSTON'S DOWNTOWN police station was in a newly renovated skyscraper. It had all the modern conveniences—telephones that were continually switched to the wrong office, elevators that went up instead of down, and parking places for everyone but the cops who needed them. John circled the block for ten minutes before he got lucky and found a space two streets over. By the time he locked his pickup and jogged back to the building, he was cussing, hot and more determined than ever to pound the truth out of Greg Lansing.

Lansing was waiting for him in one of the interrogation rooms. He looked equally unhappy.

Morgan Stacinski, the officer John had introduced to Elizabeth outside Tracy's hospital room, was waiting for John, as well. She tilted her head toward the room with the one-way mirror.

"They grabbed him at the club," she said as John walked up. "He and that character that owns it— Lyndon Kersh?—they were in Lansing's office, screaming and yelling at each other. The uniforms who picked him up said that if they'd known, they would have waited a few minutes before grabbing him. The problem might have been solved for them.''

''What do you mean?''

''Kersh had a .22 on him.''

John grinned. ''And no permit, right? Please tell me he didn't have a gun permit.''

Stace shook her head. ''He had one, but it didn't matter—'' John spoke as she did, the two of them saying it in unison ''—because they were at the club!'' Texas handgun law allowed for concealed weapons—but not where alcohol was served.

Removing his hat, John ran his fingers through his hair and shook his head. ''Hot damn, it's nice to get something right every once in a while, isn't it? Where is he?''

''Kersh is in Room 2...but so is his lawyer. C. Haden Jackson, III. You're not going to get anything from him.''

''You go on in there and work on 'em a bit, anyway,'' John said. ''I'm going to talk to Mr. Lansing.''

Lansing looked up as John pushed through the door.

''Have you been read your rights?''

The other man halfway stood, then sat back down at John's expression. ''Yes.'' He bit off the word and spat it out. ''I've been read my rights, but what the hell for, that's what I want to know.''

"Do you need an attorney? If you need an attorney and can't afford one, one will be assigned to you—"

"Cut the bullshit, Mallory! Just tell me what's going on."

John met the man's angry gaze. "You need a lawyer, Lansing."

"No, I don't."

"Okay, partner, it's your neck." John sat down on the other side of the table and opened his leather notebook, flipping to the page where he'd made notes after talking with Tracy at the hospital. When he looked up, he caught Lansing trying to decipher them upside down. "Don't strain your eyes," John said. "I'll read them to you.

"'Victim—'" he stopped and glanced up "—that's Tracy Kensington, in case there's any confusion." Lansing didn't react, and John looked back down and started to read again. "'Victim states assailant,'" he stopped once more, "and that's you, Mr. Lansing." Still no reaction. He resumed. "'...victim states assailant surprised her in parking lot at the Esquire Club on Richmond Avenue at approximately 8:00 p.m. on Sunday, August first. He proceeded to beat her about the face and head with his fists and then a blunt instrument. She believes weapon was a tire iron, but isn't sure. When he finished, he also tortured her with a cigarette lighter in an effort to get her to talk. After telling him everything she could, he left her, assuming she was dead.'''

John stopped at this point and tapped his pen against the notepad. ''Shall I keep going or have you heard enough?''

Churlish silence filled the room. John said pleasantly, ''Mr. Lansing?''

''You've got the wrong guy.''

Shaking his head, John pretended puzzlement. ''You know, we never seem to get the *right* guy into these rooms. I don't understand how that happens—especially when we manage to get so many of them into Huntsville later.'' He leaned across the table. ''And you know what? A lot of them don't ever come out.''

The man across the table sat still and silent.

John waited a moment, then spoke again. ''In Texas, capital murder gets a fellow life imprisonment or death. You know that, don't you, Mr. Lansing?''

''Capital murder! You're shittin' me! Who—''

John leaned back again. ''Miss Kensington's wallet was emptied after the beating. Somebody gets killed during a robbery, that's capital murder. Don't worry, though.'' He pointed to the bend in his arm. ''I hear you don't even feel the needle.''

Lansing's jaw twitched, and his blue eyes narrowed.

''Of course, that statute covers a second situation

we've got going on here, too.'' John flipped to the back of his notebook to a section prominently labeled 'Texas Penal Code' and began to read aloud. '' 'If multiple murders are committed during the same scheme or course of conduct, this too is capital murder.' ''

Lansing's expression shifted again, this time into disbelief. "You're crazy, Mallory! Multiple murders? I didn't try to kill Tracy, much less anyone else. Who in the hell are you talking about?''

"April Benoit, Mr. Lansing.'' John let the name rest in the stale air between them. "You killed April, and Tracy found out, so then you tried to kill her. That makes two. That's what *multiple* means. More than one.''

Lansing was shaking his head before John finished. "I didn't kill April. I swear to God I don't know anything about that.''

John didn't say a word. He just sat and stared at Greg Lansing and waited.

"Did that bitch tell you I killed April? She's lying, if she did. It wasn't me.''

"Is April dead?''

"I don't know.''

"If you didn't do it, who did?''

"I don't know. I promise, man, I don't.''

Something in Lansing's voice tipped John off in an unexpected way. He actually sounded as if he was telling the truth.

John waited until the silence built into a tangible presence in the room. "Tell me what happened. Tell me exactly how it went down, and I'll talk to the DA about the capital murder charges."

"Talk to him? What does that mean?"

"You answer the question first, *then* we'll discuss that." John stared at the man across the table. "Did you assault Tracy Kensington?"

Lansing looked toward the one-way mirror, then at the door, all the while rubbing the crook of his elbow. John wondered if he even knew what he was doing. The air-conditioning came on and a blast of frigid cold shot out of the vent above Lansing's head with a noisy *whoosh*. It seemed to jar him.

"What if I did? That doesn't mean I killed April Benoit."

John felt a flash of victory, but he pushed it away and continued. He thought he knew the answer to his next few questions, but wanted to see what the man would say. "Why did you attack Miss Kensington?"

"I didn't say I did."

"I've got your number, Lansing, so you might as well tell me the truth. You had a good reason to kill her, and I know it."

"I've got a reason, but not the one you're thinking about. She's got a big mouth and she's greedy. She sees a dollar being made she thinks she's got a right to fifty cents of it. That oughta be cause enough, right?''

John thought of the painful words Tracy had managed to speak at the hospital. She'd told him everything, but listening to Lansing, John chastised himself for not figuring it out earlier. He remembered Lansing's office. The paneled room, the big cigars, the shiny, red 'Vette Tracy had keyed when she'd gotten pissed off. Lansing didn't live at The Pines as April had, either. He rented a town house off Augusta, close to where John's own place was. The one he couldn't have afforded if his mother hadn't left it to him. If John had been thinking straighter, he would have realized what was going on before Tracy had told him.

''You've been skimming, haven't you, Lansing? Helping yourself now and then to the cash from the club? When Tracy found out, you had to stop her from telling Kersh, didn't you?'' He tapped the pen again. ''Did April know, too?''

Lansing had jerked up his head when John had begun to speak, but by the time he finished, Lansing was visibly sweating. ''I didn't kill April.''

''But Tracy knew what you were doing, didn't she? Because April told her.''

His mouth forming a thin angry line, Lansing spoke again. ''How else would she find out? She's no rocket scientist. She's not smart like April.''

''Why'd you break into April's apartment?'' John

tilted his head to Lansing's hand. The cut was healing, but the scar was still pink and puckered. "What were you looking for?"

"I kept records," he said sullenly. "I thought she might have copies at her place."

Silence filled the small tense room until John gripped the arms of his chair and tilted the chair back from the table. He crossed his arms and spoke conversationally, his voice now friendly. "You know, Greg, what I don't understand is this. Why should I believe you had nothing to do with April's disappearance? I think you tried to kill Tracy Kensington and April for the same reason. To shut them up. They both knew the same thing."

"April disappeared." Lansing held his hands out, palms up. "Just like that. One day she was there and the next day she wasn't. I don't know where she is, so I couldn't have killed her even if—" He broke off abruptly.

"Even if you wanted to?"

"Yes." The word fell like a stone.

John fought a rise of bile in his throat. A man who could beat a woman as badly as he'd beaten Tracy didn't qualify as a human being. He thought of Lansing in Elizabeth's apartment and something inside him tightened.

He let the front legs of his chair fall back, and the sound caused Lansing to jump. "And what about April's sister? What about Elizabeth? Did you tear up her town house, too, looking for the same thing? Or were you looking for *her* that night? What were your plans for her?''

''What?''

John reached across the table and grabbed a fistful of Lansing's shirt. ''Tell me the truth. What were you doing over there?''

Lansing grabbed John's hand and tried to pull it away, but John's grip wasn't budging. ''Tell me, dammit!'' he demanded, his knuckles going white with the effort of holding on. ''Why'd you trash her place?''

''I didn't! I don't know anything about it.''

''You know who Elizabeth is, though, don't you?''

''Yeah…yeah. I know who she is now. Tracy told me. She told me that night!''

''The night you beat her up?''

''I didn't—''

John dropped him so suddenly, Lansing almost fell out of his chair. ''You beat up Tracy, then you went to Elizabeth Benoit's house, didn't you?''

''No!'' He pulled on his shirt and straightened it out. ''I went home after work. That's it. Ask Brownie.''

''Brownie? The one who's lied for you already?''

''I didn't kill April and I didn't tear up her sister's place. I'm not lying!''

John sat back down and stared at the man across

the table. "What happened to April Benoit, Lansing?"

"I don't know," he said, his voice ragged. "I'm telling you the truth."

"We've got all night. You might as well tell me."

"I'd tell you if I knew."

Settling in for what he knew would be the long haul, John crossed his arms and looked over the table between them. He spoke softly, his voice as patient and low as it had been the first time he'd spoken. "I'm going to keep asking until I get a real answer, Lansing. And I've got all the time in the world. So once more, what happened to April Benoit?"

BY EIGHT that evening, Elizabeth was a nervous wreck. When they weren't checking out the window, the two officers occupied themselves with a deck of cards and a newspaper, but she had nothing except the television. She stood up from the bed where she'd been stretched out and walked aimlessly to the door of the room, then back to the bed. She thought briefly of working on Linda Tremont's case, but she'd lost her ability to concentrate. The columns would never tally, the numbers never look right.

It all seemed so unimportant now, so trivial. What did it really matter how much money Tony Masterson was taking from his wealthy clients? Elizabeth shook her head. The life-and-death issues she'd been wrestling with had a way of putting those problems, as expensive as they were, into perspective.

If only John would call! She told herself when he knew something, he'd let her know, but deep down, it wasn't just information she wanted. Dragging her feet across the carpet, she actually groaned out loud, then had to ignore the startled looks of the cops. She didn't just want news—she wanted the reassurance of his deep voice. Listening to him speak over the phone earlier had brought back the night they'd spent together with a flash of emotion and desire. She closed her eyes for a moment and recalled the feeling of putting her head against his bare chest. Hearing the rumble of his words as he'd spoken to her that night, would forever be with her. He made her feel so protected, so cared for.

After she'd made her sixth round trip to the door and back, the older of the two cops, Officer Stanley, asked, "Getting restless?"

She nodded.

He glanced at his partner. "Why don't you go get us some food? There's a good Thai place a block south of here."

The younger cop jumped immediately to his feet, then hesitated. "You'll be okay alone? I mean, I don't think I should—"

"We'll be fine," Stanley said. "Just don't take forever. And be sure to get some of that really hot chicken with lots of sauce, too."

Elizabeth watched the man leave, then stepped toward the window. She didn't pull back the drapes—they'd already warned her against that—but she peeked through the slit with one eye, confident no one could see her.

The young cop pulled away from the hotel, squealing tires accompanying his departure. With nothing else to do, she stood where she was. She couldn't see more than ten feet in either direction, but almost instantly another car backed into the slot where the police vehicle had been. The red taillights threw an eerie stripe across the sidewalk and window. It was a big car, dark brown and nondescript, and the man who got out of it looked equally unremarkable. He wore a black leather jacket over jeans and a T-shirt, a baseball cap and sunglasses.

Idly, she watched him stand outside his open car door for a moment and look around, then walk quickly to the rear of the vehicle and open the trunk. When he straightened up a moment later, he had something in his hand. She couldn't see what it was.

Stanley spoke from behind her and she jumped. He'd stood up and moved to where she was without her even knowing. Reaching out for the drapes, he apologized and said, "You might want to step away from the window, ma'am."

The words were barely out of his mouth when a sudden chill of premonition washed over Elizabeth. At that very moment the man outside whirled and looked directly at her window. Directly at *her*.

Then he raised the short-barreled gun he held— and began to fire.

"SO AFTER YOU THREW the tire iron in the bayou, where'd you go?"

Lansing stared bleary-eyed across the table at John. The room was blue with cigarette smoke, and on the table top were five plastic cups stained on the bottoms with the dregs of cold coffee. They'd been talking for hours, going over and over the same thing, step by step, word by word. There were enough slight variations in the versions for John to know Lansing was speaking the truth. Good liars never changed their stories.

"I told you already," he said raggedly. "I went straight home. I was there by midnight."

"And you didn't leave the house again that night?"

"That's right."

"And Brownie can confirm this?"

"Yes."

"Anybody else?"

Before the man could answer, a knock sounded on the door. It opened almost immediately and Morgan Stacinski stuck her head inside. She wore a noncommittal expression and didn't appear to be in a hurry, but for some reason, John instantly went on full alert.

He stood, his chair scraping the tile floor. "What is it?"

"Could you step out here for a moment, please?"

John complied, closing the door behind him. "What's wrong?"

"There's been a shooting."

"A shooting?"

"At Elizabeth's motel." Her manner was calm and professional, but her eyes filled with sympathy. "We don't have all the details yet. Stanley was hit for sure."

John knew his expression didn't change, but his heart began to pound, heavy and hard. "Was Elizabeth hurt?"

Stace shook her head. "I don't know, John. There were some civilian casualties—bystanders—but I'm not sure about her yet. It's still pretty confused, as you can imagine. Stanley's been airlifted to Hermann Hospital."

John's stomach felt as if he'd just gotten off a roller coaster. "What about Clark, the rookie? He was supposed to be with them."

"Apparently he left to go get food and when he came back, there was a gun battle going on. By the time he got his weapon out, the shooter had gone."

"Shit." John shook his head. He should have sent

someone with more experience. This was all his fault. He started down the hall, his feet on automatic pilot. "I'll go to the motel. You get on the phone and see if you can find out more about Elizabeth. Call me on my cell when you get some current info. If she's not there, I'll head for Hermann."

Almost running now to keep up with his long strides, the female detective nodded. "What about Lansing?" she said breathlessly. "Do we keep him or what?"

"Lock him up."

"And Kersh?"

They reached the hall and John stopped, punching the elevator buttons with more force than he needed. "Throw his sorry ass in another cell. Maybe they'll make some friends there." Without another word he stepped into the elevator and the doors whispered shut behind him.

Twenty minutes later he wheeled his truck into the parking lot of the motel. An ambulance with its back doors open was parked in front of what had been Elizabeth's room, and even from where he parked, John could see the damage. Ragged shards of glass hung from the front window frame, and the draperies, in tatters, were flapping in the night air, making a chilling sound. The door leading to the unit was little more than a shattered splinter of wood. A row of black holes—bullet holes—split the brick above and below the window in an almost too-neat line. Semiautomatic, he thought involuntarily. Maybe automatic. Could be a Hockler or modified Uzi.

Cold and hot at the same time, John ran through the mass of cops, emergency-medical personnel and gawking onlookers, his eyes searching the crowd. As he got closer, he saw more signs of the disaster. A woman, obviously the next-door occupant, sat on the sidewalk under her own broken window, cradling a child and sobbing. The child was crying, too, John noted, a good sign at least. A man stood nearby, a dazed expression on his face, blood streaming from cuts across his cheeks. Medics were tending to both. Reaching the battered doorway a second later, John pushed past a uniformed cop standing guard outside and ignored the man's efforts to stop him.

He stepped into the room, and what captured his gaze was the large pool of blood staining the carpet beside the window.

CHAPTER FOURTEEN

ELIZABETH SAW JOHN before he saw her and in that split second—when she witnessed the frantic expression on his face and the desperate look in his eyes—something turned over inside her and gave way. Seeing him so raw and exposed made her realize something, not just about him, but about herself, as well. How tightly she guarded her own emotions. How close to the chest she kept her own feelings. It'd been years since she'd shown the kind of passion he was revealing, and maybe even years since she'd *felt* that kind of passion.

John spotted her and crossed the room in two strides.

Elizabeth leapt up from the bed and rushed into his arms. Both began to talk at the same time.

"Are you all right? Were you hit? What happened?"

"It was horrible. I can't believe it. Thank God you're here."

They both stopped and took a breath, John's hands caressing her face as if to convince himself she was alive and well and in his arms. Then he saw the bloody splatters across her jaw and cheek, her torn shirt that had even deeper scarlet stains across it.

"Oh, God..." His gaze flew to her face. "You were hit?"

She shook her head. "No, no...it's—" The hot sting of tears filled her eyes. "It's Stanley's blood. He was shot. I was standing at the window, and he walked up and told me to move away just as I knew something was happening. He pushed me to the floor...but he took it all. There was blood everywhere." She drew a long ragged breath. "Have you heard anything about his condition? Is he..."

"I haven't seen him. I came straight here." His brown eyes turned almost black, and he tightened his grip on her arms. "Did you see the shooter, Elizabeth? Did you get a look at him?"

She nodded her head. "I did, but there's nothing I can tell you. It was dark and his face was shaded by a cap." She described the man, the car, the weapon, then shook her head. "I didn't see the gun at first, but I realized a second before he fired what was going on. I didn't know why right then, but I think it was the glasses. He was wearing sunglasses, and it was already getting dark."

"How in the hell did he find you here? No one even knew where you were staying, did they?"

She shook her head. "No," she murmured.

"After I called, you didn't call anyone, did you?"

"No."

His eyes narrowed. "This shouldn't have happened, Elizabeth. If no one knew you were here...." He seemed to close within himself for a few moments and Elizabeth could almost see him thinking. Finally he shook himself. "Are you sure you aren't hurt?"

"I'm fine," she said. "Just shaky."

His eyes held hers a moment longer, then he pulled her to him, almost roughly. For a long moment they stayed with their arms wrapped around each other, then John leaned back. "Maybe you should go to the hospital, anyway," he said gruffly, his voice thicker than it had been a moment before. "Get checked out, just to be on the safe side."

"I don't want to go anywhere." Her eyes locked on his. "I want to stay with you."

AN HOUR LATER John and Elizabeth ended up at the hospital, anyway, to learn more about Stanley. Apparently he was still in surgery.

The waiting area was a sea of blue uniforms. Cops were leaning against the walls, pacing the floor, talking in little groups. When one of their own got shot, the ranks closed in. At the center of the crowd John found Stanley's wife, Charlotte. He hugged her and let her cry, two little boys with confused looks on their faces standing uncertainly nearby. Ten minutes later he and Elizabeth left. There was nothing else they could do there.

When they reached the parking lot, John glanced over at her and swallowed hard around a painful lump in his throat. Under the yellow glow of the vapor lights, she was paler than she'd been earlier. The reality of what had happened must be catching up with her, he thought.

At the motel, when he'd realized she hadn't been hurt, something had snapped inside him. He'd known he was falling in love with her, but he hadn't realized how deep his feelings really went until he'd arrived there. God, if it had been her, if Stanley hadn't knocked her aside... John could be standing in the morgue right now, instead of the emergency room.

His fingers tightened automatically on hers, and she looked over at him in surprise.

"You're coming home with me, and I don't want any arguments."

"You aren't going to get one," she said. "I *want* to go home with you, John."

He slid his hands up her arms.

Her eyes filled with tears, and they glittered in the darkness. "I'm sorry I pulled you into this," she whispered. "I didn't know...." She stopped and shook her head. "I can't believe it started with April disappearing, and now this. A man with a wife and kids, and he's lying up there on the operating table...."

"It's his job," John said softly. "Every cop knows the risks."

The words seemed to jar her. "But—"

"We've got a bigger problem on our hands right now. We have to find out who wants you dead."

ON THE RIDE HOME John told her everything Greg Lansing had said.

Elizabeth shook her head. "I just don't understand. April never breathed a word to me about any of this. Not a word. And we talked daily."

"Maybe she didn't want you to know."

"But why?"

John glanced across the pickup cab. "Why? Look at you! You're a wreck from worrying about her and have been for weeks. If she'd told you she knew something about Greg Lansing, something he'd do anything to keep from getting out, what would you have done?"

Elizabeth let her shoulders slump, silence her only answer.

"That's right," John answered. "You would have gone crazy. *You* would have probably confronted him and then at best, you'd be the one we're looking for right now, and at worst, you'd be in the morgue."

She couldn't deny the truth. "Was that his hand I stabbed at April's apartment?"

"Yes. He wanted to see if she had any proof. He'd caught her in his office one day going through his papers, and he didn't know if she'd taken something or not, something that might implicate him later."

"But why my place? Did he think she'd brought them there?"

John exited the freeway and shook his head. "He says he didn't touch your place. Says it wasn't him. I believe him."

"But that doesn't make any sense. You said it wasn't a random thing, that the destruction was deliberate."

"I know." Turning down their street, John slowed the pickup. "And that's the part that's beginning to bug the hell out of me."

When he helped her out of the pickup, his eyes captured hers. "You okay?"

She met his gaze. "I will be."

An hour later she felt almost human again. John met her in the hallway coming out of the bathroom. "I think you should get to bed," he said. "You need to rest."

Elizabeth knew she needed rest, but she wanted to feel his arms around her more, to reassure herself she was still alive. She wanted his kisses, his touch, his breath on her skin and his mouth on hers. She wanted to ask him to take her to bed.

And so she did.

He hesitated no more than a second. Then they were in his bedroom and falling together onto the mattress.

This time it was different. They knew each other better, knew what they wanted and what felt right. John's fingers moved over her skin with a tenderness that almost made her cry. His hands smoothed her face and hair, and he couldn't seem to get enough of her. She began to realize he needed this lovemaking almost more than she. Pulling into that parking lot this evening, rushing into that motel room, not knowing if she was alive or dead....

After a little while, he seemed convinced she really was all right, and his caresses turned into something warmer and more urgent. Elizabeth reciprocated, her own touch growing bolder as it went over his chest, his arms, his stomach. Her lips followed the same route, and when she took him in her mouth, he gasped and cried her name.

She stopped the caress and shifted her body so that they lay face to face. "I want you," she said, her voice thick with desire. "Now, John... please..."

He held back and looked at her, the room too shadowed for her to read his eyes. "I want you, too, Elizabeth. But not just for now." He positioned himself over her. "Do you understand what I'm saying?"

Aching with need, the passion building inside her, she nodded and tightened her grip. "I understand."

A moment later, he plunged inside her. The rhythm built quickly. Elizabeth closed her eyes and let it take her away.

JOHN SLIPPED quietly from the bed, trying his best to move without waking Elizabeth. As the mattress creaked, she murmured once, and he held his breath, but she curled up on her side and continued to sleep, her hand tucked beneath her jaw, her hair spread out like black satin over the pillow. He stood where he was in the dawn's early shadows and stared down at her. Last night had been even more incredible than the first night they'd spent together. She was smart, beautiful and the sexiest woman he'd ever been with—the trick of fate that had gotten her into his bed and in his life was a tough one, but one thing was for sure.

He was determined to keep her there.

He padded down the hallway to the kitchen and made a pot of coffee. Then, pouring himself a mug, he carried it onto the front porch.

It hadn't even been a month since he'd watched Elizabeth go to work that day. Now their lives were irrevocably tangled, and it didn't bother him one little bit. He knew she wasn't the person he'd thought she was, walking down the sidewalk that day. He'd seen a beautiful woman and made some bad assumptions.

Thank God he'd been wrong.

But what was happening in her life? Who'd snatched her sister and was now—apparently—trying to kill her? He didn't feel any closer to an answer at this point than he'd been three weeks ago and that frustrated the hell out of him. By now he should have some solid answers. By now he should have figured things out.

He brought his mug to his mouth and sipped the hot coffee. He thought back to the suggestion he'd made to Elizabeth a few days before—that April might have planned this all herself. He'd considered it more and decided the theory didn't wash. Even if she'd had the motive, April wouldn't have been able to pull it off. From everything he'd learned about the woman, she didn't seem capable of that kind of organization.

Now, Elizabeth, she was something else. She would have been more than competent at organizing a disappearing trick. In a way she was a chameleon. In the power suits and the pulled-back hair, she was corporate America, a woman in charge of numbers and people. At the club, she had shed that skin and become a totally different person. He closed his eyes, the steam of the coffee rising up to warm his face as he remembered her on stage. She could move like smoke. The undulating sway of her hips was something most men only dreamed of, and the dark eyes behind the mask only added to the allure. He'd never seen anyone dance that way, and the memory of it, he thought, would stay with him for the rest of his life.

He opened his eyes. Who had taken her sister? Who wanted to kill her?

Where would it all end?

WHEN ELIZABETH WOKE up, John had already left, but the note beside the bed told her he'd be back by lunch. She stretched, her body still tingling from the night before.

With John's robe—at least four sizes too big—around her Elizabeth made her way down the hall-way. His note had told her to expect cops in the kitchen, and cops there were. Two officers sat read-ing the morning paper and sipping cups of coffee. They looked up as she entered the room and smiled, introducing themselves to her. They were both older men with gazes so sharp she was glad she was on the right side of the law.

After a few moments of small talk, they went back to perusing the news, interrupted with frequent stares out the kitchen window.

She filled a mug with coffee and went back down the hall. She took her time bathing and dressing, and before she knew it the morning was almost over.

When the phone rang around eleven, she dropped the book she'd been reading and jumped up quickly to grab the receiver, expecting John's deep voice.

It was Linda Tremont. "I hope I'm not interrupting anything," she said. "But I read about what happened in the paper this morning and I couldn't believe it. I called your office, and they told me I could reach you at this number. Are you okay?"

"I'm fine," Elizabeth answered. "I can't believe it made the *Chronicle*, though."

"Sounds as if you've been having a pretty rough time." Her voice was so sympathetic, Elizabeth's eyes welled up. "Can I do anything?"

"I appreciate the offer, Linda, but right now there's nothing anyone can do."

"Still no word on April?"

"Absolutely nothing."

"God, I'm sorry, and even sorrier that I have to bring this up, but I don't know what else to do. I was wondering if you'd finished the report yet. It sounded like you were getting close to being done the last time we talked, but I wasn't sure...."

"I wrote a preliminary outline, but along with everything else that's been going on, my home was totally trashed last week. I had to throw away reams of things, and I haven't had a chance to go through the papers I managed to salvage. I don't know if the report survived or not."

"Oh, I'm sorry, Elizabeth." There was a pause

before she spoke again, hesitantly. "I don't know what to do, then. Tony's had a change of heart and he wants to talk to the S.E.C. about the situation. If we don't act fast…"

"I could call them and set up an appointment."

"I've already done that, but the agent in charge said he really needs your report first." She paused. "I hate to be a pain, Elizabeth, but I'm scared to death Tony's going to back out. I don't know where you are right now, but what if we met at your place and I helped you look through your papers? Would that work? I want to get this over with—for Tony's sake."

The thought of focusing on something else for a few hours suddenly sounded like an excellent idea. "Sure. How soon can you get here?"

John called a few minutes later. "I'm at the hospital," he said when Elizabeth answered. "Stanley might be able to talk to me in a little while and I need to get his statement. Are you doing okay?"

"We're fine," she said. She closed her eyes for a moment and savored the sound of his voice and all it brought with it. "When do you think you might get here?"

His voice dropped an octave. "Do you miss me?"

She laughed lightly. "Well, actually, yes, I do, but that's not why I'm asking. Linda Tremont read about the shooting in the paper. She's meeting me at my town house so we can go through my papers.''

''Damn. I thought there for a second I might be making some headway with you.''

She hesitated, her own voice husky when she spoke. ''You *are* making headway with me,'' she said. ''Maybe more than you want.''

''*More* than I want? That's not possible,'' he said. ''I meant what I said last night, Elizabeth. This isn't a temporary thing for me. I want you in my life—and in Lisa's.''

Elizabeth swallowed. ''That sounds like a commitment to me.''

''Call it anything you like. I want us together, though. That's what I'm saying.''

''I understand.''

''That's what you said last night,'' he answered softly. ''Do you just understand…or do you want it, too?''

Elizabeth gripped the phone. ''I don't know,'' she said honestly. ''It's been a long time since I considered that kind of thing.''

''Since you *let* yourself consider it.''

''Maybe.''

''It *could* happen.''

''I know.''

Silence built over the line as Elizabeth thought about his words. When it became obvious she didn't know exactly how to reply, John changed the subject.

"Be careful, okay? Don't go anywhere else but your town house but take McCurry with you."

"Okay."

She started to hang up, then John spoke her name. She brought the receiver back to her ear. "Yes?"

"I meant what I said. Be careful. I can only handle one shoot-out a week."

They laughed together, then hung up, but underneath the humor, Elizabeth had heard the concern. He loved her. He wanted them to share a life, a home and a family. Hearing the promise in his voice made Elizabeth feel warm and wonderful.

It also made her want to run and hide.

CHAPTER FIFTEEN

LINDA ARRIVED shortly after that, and the two women met on the porch at Elizabeth's town house. One of the officers trailed along behind. When they reached the front door, he unlocked it and told them to wait.

While they paused in the warm sunshine, Elizabeth studied Linda. The woman looked much worse than the last time she'd seen her. Her skin was a sickly shade of green, and lines that hadn't been there before now crisscrossed her forehead and puckered her mouth. Her suit was wrinkled and sported a stain near the hem. She fussed nervously with the strap of her purse, her eyes darting over her shoulder several times to her car in the parking lot. Her brother's situation was obviously taking a toll on her.

Elizabeth spoke quietly. "I'm sorry all this trouble with your brother has happened, Linda. You don't deserve this kind of mess."

Her startled eyes blinked rapidly. "Wh-what?"

"You can't fix other people's problems, even if you are related to them. He's a grown man who's got to take care of his own situations and not involve you in them all the time. It's not your responsibility to make things right when he's screwed them up.''

As soon as she'd said the words, Elizabeth realized how foolish they sounded coming from her own mouth. She'd done the same thing, hadn't she? Whenever April had goofed up, who'd been there trying to make it all right again? Suddenly it seemed so clear.... Had she really thought she was helping her sister? The reality was she'd been doing just the opposite, hobbling her with kindness, keeping her dependent, instead of letting her fall and get up on her own.

How could she have been so blind?

The answer to that question came just as quickly as her revelation had. Elizabeth had *needed* to be the one who fixed things. She'd done it for so long—for April, for their mother, for herself—that letting anyone else be in charge had become unthinkable. Only now, with John's help, did she realize it wasn't necessary. She'd been coming to this truth over the course of the past month, but now, all at once, she understood herself as she never had before.

She felt as if a great weight had been lifted from her shoulders. For a moment she thought she might float away, then the voice of the officer brought her back down.

"It's okay, ladies," he said. "You can go on in. I'll be waiting on the porch if you need me."

Her brain spinning, Elizabeth stepped into the house with Linda. She stood there for a second, still thinking, then Linda asked, "Where are they, Elizabeth? The papers?"

"They're in the den," she said. She turned and began to walk down the hall. "There really wasn't much left, but I thought I should keep them and go through them later." Without looking behind her, she entered the small study and walked directly to a row of cardboard boxes lining one wall. "We can start here," she said, "and work our way down. They're not in any kind of order."

Elizabeth lifted the lid off the first box, and when there was no response from Linda, she turned.

The reason for her silence was immediately obvious. "Please don't make this difficult," Linda said calmly as she raised her gun.

THE DOCTORS gave John ten minutes to talk to the wounded officer, but he could have had ten hours and it wouldn't have helped. Stanley managed to croak out even fewer details than Elizabeth had provided. He hadn't seen the shooter at all. The draperies had exploded, and he'd gone down. He knew nothing beyond that.

Discouraged and frustrated, John left the hospital

and went to see the one person who could make him think the clearest. His daughter.

On the way to Marsha's house, though, he called home just to check.

The cop who answered the phone had a west-Texas accent. "Everythang's jes' fine, Detective. She's at her place, 'long with that woman who came to see her. And McCurry went inside first to check thangs out. He's out front watching the place. I can see 'im from here."

John ended the call and kept driving.

Marsha was at work, as he'd known she would be. The housekeeper answered the door, then stepped aside as he entered without for waiting for her approval.

He swept his hat off and spoke. "I'd like to see my daughter. Where is she?"

The older woman straightened her shoulders and glared at him. "I'm sorry, sir, but Mrs. Mallory left me no instructions about you seeing Lisa today."

"She is no longer Mrs. Mallory," he said, interrupting her with a level stare of his own. "And you can phone her if you like, but I'm here, I only have a few moments, and I'm seeing my daughter whether you like it or not. Where is she?"

She pursed her lips but answered. "Upstairs in her room. I'll show you—"

"I can find her." He turned on his heel and started up the staircase, going left when he hit the top. On the right was the bedroom he and Marsha had shared, and he was suddenly glad he didn't have to walk past the scene of that crime. They'd had so many fights in there, it was all he could remember. No tenderness, no fun, and certainly none of the sexual fireworks he'd shared with Elizabeth.

He knocked on Lisa's open door and she turned away from the dollhouse she'd been rearranging. An enormous grin split her face and she yelled, "Daddy!" Catapulting into his arms, she rained a series of kisses over his face and chin. "Ohhh, you're sticky!" she cried, rubbing her hand over his stubble. "You need to shave!"

"Well, I love you, too," he said with a grin. He swung her around once, then kneeled and put her down, keeping his arms around her. "I only have a minute, but I had to come see my baby. How ya doin'?"

"I'm not a baby," she said. "I'm a big girl."

"I know that," he said. "But daddies always think of their little girls as babies. That's just how it goes."

"Well, when I grow up I'm gonna be a beautiful lady just like Elizabeth."

John grinned again, then she tugged at his hand. "Come see my new dollhouse. It's got furniture and windows and everything."

He let her lead him across the carpet to the miniature home. He folded his long legs to sit on the floor beside her and look into the tiny windows. She chattered without drawing a breath, pointing out all the details to him. Launching next into a full-scale history of each tiny figure in the home, she explained the complicated relationships of everyone in the place. Half the stuff she was saying sounded as if it'd come straight from the soaps—something he was sure she was not supposed to watch, but which, he suspected, the old battle-ax downstairs probably let her get away with because she watched them herself.

John nodded and smiled and asked all the right questions, but the back of his brain was doing what he'd wanted. Working on Elizabeth's problem.

"And this is Mindy. She's married to Luke but she got something called 'nesia and she doesn't know who she is." She held up a tiny figure and beamed. "This is Michael. He and Luke are twins. They look 'xactly alike and sometimes they pretend to be each other so Mindy can't really tell the difference so sometimes she gets confused and..."

With less than half an ear, he listened to it all, but somehow, through the fog of his thinking, her patter reached him. The words, so meaningless a moment before, took on a significance that stole his breath. He stared at Lisa, a numb feeling of disbelief starting in his gut and working its way up.

His astonishment must have shown on his face.

"What is it, Daddy? You look funny. Are you sick?"

"No, honey. I'm fine. I...I'm just thinking. You go ahead and tell me the rest of the story. I'm listening."

Reassured, she continued talking, acting out the parts with the tiny dolls she held in her hands. But John *wasn't* listening. He was thinking, thinking back to that day he'd watched Elizabeth walk to her car. She'd had on a black suit and low heels, her hair pulled back, sunglasses perched on her nose. It'd been close to 6:00 a.m. He always got up at a quarter till, fixed his coffee, then walked to the window. By 6:00 a.m. he was staring outside.

He'd never seen her leave before. Prior to that day, he'd seen her at the pool, he'd seen her at the mailboxes, he'd seen her going to her car...but never that early.

And now he realized why.

He hadn't seen Elizabeth. He'd seen April.

Dressed in what were Elizabeth's clothes, carrying a purse of hers, wearing her hair—probably newly dyed—pulled back just as Elizabeth wore it, April had switched identities with her sister. That's why the police had found one of Elizabeth's shoes in the Mercedes. April had been wearing them.

He'd seen April and assumed it was Elizabeth.

Just as her abductor had.

His pulse took that jump it always did when things finally clicked into place, when the last puzzle piece was set on the board and the picture became apparent. He'd been going at it the wrong way entirely. This had never been about April at all. Whoever had grabbed her had thought they were getting Elizabeth. They'd been after her all along—April had just got in the way.

He leapt to his feet. "Daddy's gotta go, baby," he said, pulling her to him and hugging her tight. "But I'll see you on Thursday just like always, okay?"

She hugged him back. "Okay."

Cramming his hat on his head, he ran down the stairs, jumped in his truck and took off.

ELIZABETH STARED at the gun, then raised her eyes to Linda's face. Her skin looked hot and feverish, but the gleam in her eyes was chilling. "Wh-what are you doing?"

"I'm taking care of my brother," Linda answered calmly. "I don't care what you said in your little speech on the front porch. I love Tony, and it *is* my responsibility to help him. He tried to fix things at the motel, but it didn't work out."

"Th-that was Tony? My God, Linda, why? How—"

"You phoned me, remember? I have caller ID and I looked up the number in a reverse directory.

It gave me the name, and I told Tony where you were. He was watching afterward, and he saw you and your policeman lover. He followed you to the hospital, then waited and trailed you here."

Elizabeth moaned. "But why? I don't understand."

"He's a good boy, Elizabeth, he really is."

The words were spoken with perfect tranquility. She seemed calm and collected now that she had the gun in her hand. Elizabeth swallowed, her throat convulsing with fear. "Linda, he shot a policeman. A man with a family."

"It was the only way. I told him to do it."

"But why?"

"Why? Because your sister's an idiot, that's why," she said coldly. "That's also why you were always having to get her out of dilemmas, but Tony's brilliant, so brilliant he's always been misunderstood. I've had to help him because no one else could. No one else appreciated him. He tried to take care of things himself, but he made a mistake— an honest mistake that anyone would have in the same position." Her face contorted suddenly. "It was *her* fault! She was dressed in your clothes. She looked like you."

Elizabeth's knees suddenly weakened as the pieces fell into place. Her missing car. The shoe. "Are you telling me your brother t-took my sister, thinking it was me?"

"Yes."

Elizabeth flinched, cold, dreaded fear stopping her heart. A faint buzz sounded in her ears. "Did he...did he kill her?"

The woman before her spoke as if Elizabeth hadn't said a word. "This is all your fault, you know. If you hadn't written that stupid report—"

"That's my job, Linda!"

"You could have helped us out a little. Waited to tell the S.E.C. Tony would have fixed it. All he needed was a little time. He wanted to tell you what his plan was and explain how it was going to work."

Elizabeth stared at the woman, frozen with shock. The gun trembled in Linda's hand and she made a sound that might have passed for a laugh in different circumstances. "He thought he was getting *you.* She came out of your town house, wearing one of your suits, with her hair black and slicked back. He'd been waiting to grab you." She frowned. "He just wanted to tell you how the funds had gotten messed up, and he knew you wouldn't listen to him unless he took you someplace quiet and forced you to hear what he had to say."

Elizabeth blinked. "She was dressed like me? That doesn't make sense. Why would she do that?"

Linda waved the gun, and Elizabeth recoiled. "Who knows? Who cares? The only important thing is that report. Where is it, Elizabeth? I know you've got it hidden somewhere here. Tony turned this place upside down and he couldn't locate it. I don't want it found when they discover your body.''

The words registered dimly. Tony had trashed her home, getting in, she realized now, with April's keys. Blinking, Elizabeth held out both her hands. ''Listen to me, Linda. There's a cop watching this place from John's town house. And another one is on the front porch. If you shoot me, there's no way you're getting out of this.''

''So?''

''Y-you don't care?''

''Tony is my life. If I kill you, the S.E.C. will never know anything, and that's the only thing I care about. I've got to protect him.''

''Who'll protect him if you're in jail?''

The question seemed to stop her. ''I...I'll worry about that later.''

''Linda, you're not thinking straight. Put down the gun and let's talk this out. Otherwise you and your brother both are going to end up in prison. Kidnapping is a federal offense, and—'' Elizabeth licked her dry lips ''—and if he's killed April, he'll get the death penalty for sure. You can shoot me, but the truth will come out. It always does.''

Linda's fingers tightened on the gun. ''I love my brother,'' she said quietly, ''and if you think I'd let him go to prison, you're crazy. I'll kill everyone in sight before I let that happen...and I'll start right here with you.''

HIS STEPS MUFFLED by Elizabeth's thick carpet, John was just about to call out when he heard voices. As he got closer to the room, the words became distinct.

''...I'll kill everyone in sight...and I'll start right here with you.''

He didn't recognize the voice, but he didn't care. His hand snaked inside his coat and pulled out his gun. In the filtered light of the hallway, the gleaming blue-black barrel of the .44 Magnum was rock-steady.

''Linda, this isn't the way to do this. Please. Let me help you. We can figure something out.''

Elizabeth was clearly terrified, but he had to admire her. Not too many people would have sounded that calm after hearing such a threat. He continued down the tiny hall, his gun pointed upward, his boots gliding soundlessly on the carpet.

''There's nothing to discuss. Find that report.''

''I—I'm not even sure it's here. It might have gotten thrown out.''

''Don't lie to me, Elizabeth. It won't do you any good.''

John stopped. His back against the wall, he was just outside the doorway. He took two deep breaths, counted to three, then swung around, his weapon pointed out, chest-high, his deep voice booming and filling the tiny room. "Drop the gun! Drop it now!"

LATER, Elizabeth would play the scene out in her head. Sometimes it happened fast, as if in speeded-up time, and sometimes it happened slowly, like a film being shown frame by frame. But at the very moment, when it actually took place, all she felt was relief at seeing John—then horror as Linda fired over Elizabeth's shoulder. Right into John's chest.

Blocked by Elizabeth's body, he hadn't seen where Linda was pointing the gun. He staggered backward and crashed into the wall behind him. Elizabeth screamed and ran toward him, realizing at once that he had on a bulletproof vest. Before she could reach him, though, Linda fired again, the sound of the gun deafening, the smell of the powder overwhelming.

Elizabeth's eyes locked on John's. He was moving his mouth, but she didn't understand him. She couldn't even hear his words. He reached out, pulled her to him, then fired over her head. The shot reverberated in the tiny room, and Elizabeth twisted around just in time to see Linda fall.

She whipped her head back. John's expression was so shocked that she shivered, a sudden sweep of coldness coming over her. She followed his horrified gaze and looked down.

Her blouse had turned crimson. She reached out and pulled it away from her skin. It was wet and sticky and red, and finally, pain crashing over her simultaneously, she understood.

She'd been shot.

She looked up at him then her world went dark.

JOHN SAT outside the operating room, his head in his hands. For the first time in his career, he'd sent other officers to make the arrest. A wounded Linda Tremont had told them where her brother was, and John had dispatched them without him. All he could think about was Elizabeth. The doctors wheeling her into surgery had only yelled at him to get out as they'd rushed her by. "We'll let you know as soon as we can."

How many times had he said those same damn words to someone else? To a mother waiting for the murderer of her child to be found. To the man waiting for his lawyer to show up. To a defendant waiting for a verdict. They took on a whole new meaning when you were hearing them, instead of speaking them.

He closed his eyes and began to pray.

ELIZABETH THOUGHT she was dreaming. She heard April's voice, coming to her through a fog, and felt the warmth of her sister's touch.

"I love you, Lizzie. I've never really told you, but I should have. All I did was give you a hard time, and I'm sorry. If I ever get a second chance,

I promise, you'll always know what you mean to me." The imaginary fingers tightened. "I just wanted to take care of things by myself for once. That's it. I wanted to solve this problem without asking you for help because...well, I'm going to have a baby, Elizabeth. I'm going to be a mother and it's time for me to grow up."

Elizabeth wanted to answer, to say something about April's news, but her muscles wouldn't work and she couldn't force the words through her throat. It didn't matter one way or the other, she thought groggily. It was just a dream.

After a little while, another voice sounded, this one deeper, throbbing against her consciousness, almost willing her to wake. It was John, of course. "I love you, Elizabeth. You know that, don't you? You're the only woman in the world I want."

Again she tried to answer. "I love you, too," she wanted to say, but the words just wouldn't come.

Later—it could have been days, it could have been hours, she didn't know—the dream voice came back, the words going in and out before they began to disappear completely. Elizabeth heard the last plaintive question, and tears came into her eyes at the lost tones and despondent manner.

"Can you ever forgive me, Elizabeth? Ever, ever in a million years?"

IT DIDN'T HAPPEN as it did in the movies. Elizabeth didn't come into consciousness slowly or through a blurry mist of confusion. One minute she was asleep, and the next she was awake. Fully awake. She opened her eyes.

April stood on one side of the bed, John on the other.

They stared at her and she stared at them...then everyone began to talk at once. Laughing and crying, April threw her arms around Elizabeth and hugged her, careful of her bandaged chest. John nudged her aside and did the same. Then they each took one of Elizabeth's hands.

Elizabeth blinked tears away and stared at her sister. "You're here," she said, shaking her head and staring at April. "Really here. I...I thought I was dreaming." She turned and looked at John, her fingers gripping his so hard she was sure she must be hurting him. "Where did you find her?"

"Linda told us everything after she shot you. Masterson was not in Europe—he was keeping April at his house on Lake Conroe. The SWAT team went up there and got April an hour after Linda confessed."

Elizabeth turned back to April, her eyes roaming her face as if she still couldn't believe it; her twin was here. "Are you all right? He didn't hurt you, did he? The blood in the car—where'd that come from?"

April held up her arm. On the underside was a

small white bandage. "He had a knife. That's how he forced me to go with him. He sliced me, but it was superficial. I cleaned it up myself once we got to his house. It's fine now." April smiled and shook her head. "You'll never stop, will you? You'll always be mothering me, won't you?"

Elizabeth's voice was husky from the sting of tears. "I...I guess." She turned to look at John. "Oh, God...how can I ever thank you?"

Before he could reply, April spoke. "You?" She tugged on Elizabeth's hand. "I think *I'm* the one who needs to be thanking the man, don't you?" Without waiting for Elizabeth to answer, April smiled at John. "And I already *have* thanked him. About a thousand times."

Over Elizabeth's battered body, something passed between her sister and the man Elizabeth loved, some kind of understanding on his part, a wave of appreciation on hers. When April's eyes met Elizabeth's, there was no mistaking the message.

You found him first. He's all yours.

"I had the weirdest dream," Elizabeth said after a few seconds. "I dreamed we were talking and you told me you were going to have a baby."

"It wasn't a dream," April said quietly. "I am pregnant."

Elizabeth's mouth dropped open. "Oh, my God! Are you serious?"

April nodded. "Three months' worth of serious.

It's one of the reasons I did what I did. I shouldn't be depending on you if I'm bringing someone else into the world. I woke up and realized it's time for me to depend on me. When I turned up pregnant, reality hit. Finally.''

"And the baby's father?" John asked. "You can't depend on him?"

"No." Her voice was sharp but determined. "That's not an option."

Stunned by the rapid turn of events, Elizabeth could only stare at her sister. A million questions filled her head, but the tone with which April had answered John revealed there might be fewer answers. Which was all right, Elizabeth told herself. April *was* an adult. But Elizabeth had to ask once more. "Are you really all right? And the baby's okay?"

"We're both fine. When Tony realized he'd grabbed me instead of you, he went berserk. His sister's the one I was afraid of, though."

"But why were you dressed like me?" Elizabeth shook her head and looked at April. "Why, sweetheart?"

April sighed and looked out the window. "Oh, Elizabeth, it was dumb, I know that now. But like I said, with the baby coming, I wanted so badly to get out of a problem for once without you having to get involved." She looked back down at the bed. "I knew Greg was stealing Kersh blind by skimming cash at the club, and Greg *knew* I knew. I thought if I went to him pretending to be you that I could get him to leave me alone. Threaten him with some kind of obscure law or something." She rolled her eyes. "It was stupid, really, really stupid, but it seemed to be the only way at the time. I...I wanted to prove to you I could take care of myself, and the only way I knew how to do that was to pretend to *be* you."

Emotion gripped Elizabeth's heart and wouldn't let it go. "Oh, sweetheart, you *can* take care of yourself—and without pretending to be me. You're smart and beautiful and—"

"And an idiot." April's gaze, unusually serious, met Elizabeth's. "All this was my fault. Tracy—you—the cop—everything." She glanced at John, interrupting herself. "Are you sure Tracy will be okay?"

"She's going to have a rough time, but the doctors think she'll make it. Stanley, too."

April nodded once, then turned back to Elizabeth. "It was all my fault, but things are going to change," she promised. "They already have."

"I love you no matter what," Elizabeth said thickly. "Changed, the same, whatever. It doesn't matter. And I already love your baby."

April's gaze shimmered with tears, and Elizabeth turned to John, too emotional to say more to her sister. "Where's Linda?" she asked, changing the subject. "Is she..."

"She's on the floor beneath you, under guard." He shook his head. "She should never have been able to get that close to you to begin with. I should have realized what was going on when you told me she read about the shooting in the paper. It wasn't *in* the paper."

His dark eyes were filled with concern and love. He leaned closer to her and drew a finger down her cheek. If she wanted to escape emotions, this wasn't the time or the place. Her heart closed in on itself as she looked into his eyes. "This is my fault, Elizabeth, and it never should have happened."

"It's no one's fault but Linda's." She reached up and put her hand on his face. "You saved me."

"And *you* scared the hell outta me. I thought there for a minute I'd lost you and—"

April coughed. "I think I'll step outside."

She started to move away from the bed, but Elizabeth stopped her. "April..." Their eyes met, two gazes so similar and yet so different. Elizabeth's relief and love was so overwhelming she felt dizzy with it. "I don't know how to tell you how glad I am you're okay. I love you."

April nodded. "I know. I've always known that, but I didn't realize how much until now. I'm a very lucky woman to have such a wonderful sister." Their look said it all, then April left.

Elizabeth turned back to John, her throat clogged with emotion. "I'm serious," she said. "I'll never be able to thank you for what you did. Never."

He smiled his devastating smile. "I can think of a lot of ways you could thank me. But we'll just start with this." Leaning closer to her once again, he pressed his lips to hers in a kiss so gentle she could hardly feel it. It was enough, though. A thrill ran through her, especially when she saw the love shining in his eyes.

"Elizabeth," he said quietly, "I knew I loved you before you got shot, but when that happened, right smack in front of my eyes, I thought I was going to die myself."

"I love you, too," she said softly. "Because you've made me realize what that really means. Love is not just taking care of someone, it's letting them be themselves. And still loving them." She smiled. "Warts and all."

He smiled back, his brown eyes filling her with hope for the future. "Honey, if you have any warts, I haven't seen them."

She wrapped her good arm around his neck and pulled him a little closer. "I think there're a few places you haven't looked yet. I might be a terrible aunt…or a really bad mother."

"I don't think so," he said. "Lisa's already told me she wants to be a beautiful lady just like you. I'm sure she'd love for you to be her stepmother."

Stepmother? Her? The thought—and all its implications—choked Elizabeth even more and this time the tears really fell.

But John stopped them with his thumbs, his touch one of featherlike tenderness. She knew then how utterly wrong she'd been. The kind of love that had brought them together, and that she was feeling right now was nothing short of a miracle. Why had she been so afraid? She didn't have an answer to that question, but she didn't need one. John had answered it for her in the best possible way....

* * * * *

For a change of pace,
try Kay David's romantic comedy,

TOO HOT FOR COMFORT.

On sale May 2000
from Harlequin Duets.

If you enjoyed what you just read,
then we've got an offer you can't resist!

Take 2 bestselling love stories FREE!

Plus get a FREE surprise gift!

Clip this page and mail it to Harlequin Reader Service®

IN U.S.A.	IN CANADA
3010 Walden Ave.	P.O. Box 609
P.O. Box 1867	Fort Erie, Ontario
Buffalo, N.Y. 14240-1867	L2A 5X3

YES! Please send me 2 free Harlequin Supperromance® novels and my free surprise gift. Then send me 6 brand-new novels every month, which I will receive months before they're available in stores. In the U.S.A., bill me at the bargain price of $3.57 plus 25¢ delivery per book and applicable sales tax, if any*. In Canada, bill me at the bargain price of $3.96 plus 25¢ delivery per book and applicable taxes**. That's the complete price, and a saving of over 10% off the cover prices—what a great deal! I understand that accepting the 2 free books and gift places me under no obligation ever to buy any books. I can always return a shipment and cancel at any time. Even if I never buy another book from Harlequin, the 2 free books and gift are mine to keep forever. So why not take us up on our invitation. You'll be glad you did!

135 HEN CQW6
336 HEN CQW7

Name _____ (PLEASE PRINT) _____

Address _____ Apt.# _____

City _____ State/Prov. _____ Zip/Postal Code _____

---

* Terms and prices subject to change without notice. Sales tax applicable in N.Y.
** Canadian residents will be charged applicable provincial taxes and GST.
   All orders subject to approval. Offer limited to one per household.
   ® is a registered trademark of Harlequin Enterprises Limited.

6SUP99   ©1998 Harlequin Enterprises Limited

Come escape with Harlequin's new

Series Sampler

Four great full-length Harlequin novels bound together in one fabulous volume and at an unbelievable price.

Be transported back
in time with a
Harlequin Historical®
novel, get caught up
in a mystery with Intrigue®,
be tempted by a hot, sizzling romance
with Harlequin Temptation®,
or just enjoy a down-home
all-American read with
American Romance®.

You won't be able to put this collection down!

On sale February 2000 at your favorite retail outlet.

HARLEQUIN®
Makes any time special ™

HARLEQUIN®
SUPERROMANCE®

Pregnant...and
on her own?

HER BEST FRIEND'S BABY by **C.J. Carmichael**
(Superromance #891)
Mallory and Drew are best friends—and then they share an
unexpected night of passion. Mallory's pregnant.... Being
"just friends" again is impossible. Which leaves being lovers—
or getting married.
On sale January 2000

EXPECTATIONS by **Brenda Novak**
(Superromance #899)
Jenna's pregnant by her abusive ex-husband. Her first love,
Adam, comes back on the scene, wanting to reconcile. Will he still
want her when he learns she's pregnant with another man's child?
On sale February 2000

BECAUSE OF THE BABY by **Anne Haven**
(Superromance #905)
They're friends and colleagues. One hot summer night, Melissa
and Kyle give in to the secret attraction they've never acknowledged.
It's changed their lives forever—because Melissa is pregnant.
On sale March 2000

Available at your favorite retail outlet.

HARLEQUIN®
Makes any time special ™

Visit us at www.romance.net

HSR9ML00